Above the Ashes

Book One of the Blood and Hexes Trilogy

by
ALEXANDER FERNANDEZ

Edited by
Trana M. Simmons

Book One: Above the Ashes
Book Two: Below the Darkness
Book Three: Through the Heavens and Earth

Chapter One

Plymouth, England 1689

Frantic hands shook Sybil until she woke to her mother's pale, terrified face in the light of an oil lamp.

"Wake up, daughter! Danger is upon us, and the time for our voyage hath come."

The grogginess vanished as Sybil flew out of bed. Aware of the reason for her mother's distress, Sybil sped into her well-trained repetition. Her heart pounded despite the number of times she had practiced for this very moment.

Fear trembled her body as she slipped into her gray mantua with elbow-length, cuffed sleeves. Having a great need for haste, no rigid bodice or cumbersome, overlapping skirts would be worn tonight. Dressed, she quickly collected her light brown hair into an unkempt bun, then lifted the hem of her dress to slip on her footwear.

She joined her mother near the entrance of the cottage, and together they hefted a wooden trunk through the doorway. Chill night air rose goosebumps on Sybil's skin. The white moon contrasted against the dark sky, a brilliant chip of ice in a black sea. Out of breath from the heavy load, her mother struggled on the opposite handle of the trunk. Sybil grunted as they hoisted the chest into the back of an uncovered wagon strapped to a pair of horses. A grim-faced, bearded man in a soiled waistcoat and breeches perched in the front seat. He stared at Sybil and her mother with no obvious intention of helping.

Sybil turned to go back into the house, but her mother's grip stopped her. "I fear there is no time for anything else, daughter. Mr. Chandler hath warned me that the witch-hunters are riding hither. We only have a short time to reach the pier, I warrant."

The witch-hunters. As the driving force behind the Pendle witch trials of 1612, the forefathers of this murderous organization had executed Sybil's great-grandmother and nine other individuals for practicing witchcraft in Lancashire. Since then, the Cotterills—Sybil's family—had moved out of Lancashire to Coventry, London, and eventually Plymouth in lower England while avoiding persecution over the years. They had always practiced in secret having one eye on their craft and the other glancing out the window in trepidation. Sybil's mother, Olivia, had trained her daughter well not only in magic, but also in preparation for escape on a night such as this.

Sybil climbed into the back of the wagon and extended an arm to pull her mother aboard. Seated uncomfortably on wooden boards, the pair leaned on the hard trunk and held each other's hands. The wagon lurched into motion as the horses clomped on the dirt road.

"Do the Chandlers fare well?" Sybil asked. She had met their family on occasion ever since moving to

Plymouth. As witches, the Chandlers also faced great peril with hunters in pursuit.

"My heart hopes," said Olivia. "Their daughter, Constance, shall meet us at yonder pier."

Sybil leaned in close to her mother. "Truly, are we safe with this strange man taking us?"

"We shall be safer than with aforesaid witch-hunters," Olivia replied. "He conceives what we are, but money is all he cares about. He is a dockhand, and arrangements for our passage to the New England Colonies are set forthwith. We shall be sailing aboard the *John of London*."

Longing swept over Sybil as she stared at the cottage disappearing in the night. She had known this moment would arrive eventually. However, the mental and physical preparation couldn't subdue the fear and sorrow caused by the abrupt reality of having to leave everything behind while running for her life.

Olivia caressed Sybil's cheek and forehead. Her sweet smile cleared some of the gloom in Sybil's heart. "Your young face says it all, my daughter. This is happening too fast and not what either of us desired. But leaving England is the best plan, I warrant. The cottage where our family dwelt is so full of loving memories that shall never disappear. After your father passed away years agone, he continued to take care of us hitherto by providing a comfortable home and a good life. You are only fifteen and have been educated as much as possible. Of a truth, you are an adept witch, and forthwith we have a chance to begin a new life in yonder Colonies."

Sybil wiped her teary eyes and smiled at her mother, a beautiful woman despite a tousled appearance from rushing out the door in the middle of the night. Her dark eyes glittered beneath the moon. Passing shadows from surrounding trees enhanced the smooth contours of her face. Strength and determination also shone in Olivia's expression. Sybil latched onto that courage, the same maternal resilience that had protected her for so many years. Feeling better, she swore she would not be a burden to her mother on this journey.

"Truly, I am happy to be with you no matter where we dwell," said Sybil.

"As I am with you, sweet one," Olivia replied.

She removed a necklace tucked inside her dress and unfastened the clasp, then held it up in the jostling wagon. The chain attached to a silver pentacle, a talisman containing an encircled five-pointed star, a symbol of ancient and mystical power. She reached behind Sybil's neck and secured the jewelry in place.

"Mother, I cannot. This is yours—"

"Exactly. Thus, it is mine to give away as a gift to my only daughter. This once belonged to your great-grandmother. She passed the necklace to my mother, and forthwith I give it unto you."

The cool metal pressed against Sybil's chest, its weight filled with a long history of love, lineage, and enchanted properties. She vowed to protect the necklace until…would she ever have a child to pass it onto?

She leaned forward and wrapped her mother in a fervent hug. "I love you, Mother."

"I love you, too." Olivia pulled back and stroked Sybil's hair. "My beautiful baby. You have eyes the color of afternoon tea, and hair the color of fresh baked biscuits."

Sybil smiled. "I fancy some of both forthwith."

Holding each other for some warmth, mother and daughter tried to make themselves as comfortable as possible during the rest of the slow, rough ride to the docks. Sybil glanced at the man's back as he guided the horses. Were they really as safe as her mother had said? And what exactly had been the arrangements? The man never turned around or said a word. He only snapped the reins and swigged from a brown bottle the entire way.

"We have arrived," Olivia finally said.

The wagon departed the uneven dirt road and rumbled onto a stretch of cobblestone. Sybil inhaled the salty ocean air and listened to water lapping around the wooden posts of the pier ahead. The cobblestone ended and the spoked wheels of the wagon rolled across a moist network of planks and crossbeams making up the Plymouth harbor.

The bearded man halted the horses and jumped off the wagon to speak with another male holding a lamp. Sybil and her mother had to pull down the heavy trunk. The labor done, Sybil observed three sailing vessels moored to the long wharf. "Is one of yonder ships the *John of London*?"

"Yes, the one in the middle," Olivia answered. "However, it is not set to sail until the morrow, and we are not on the passenger list. Our names ought to remaineth hidden, as using Cotterill may be unwise after what happened in Lancashire with your great-grandmother. I warrant our ancestry is how these hunters located us around the country and eventually came upon us hither. Most people are terrified of witches and do not care to understand what we are. We have always traveled to avoid attention, and it would behoove us to leave the country unrecognized. The Colonies give us hope by leaving the witch-hunting in England behind."

Anxious, Sybil clutched the necklace through the front of her dress. "If we are not on the list, how shall we get onboard?"

"The man who brought us shall take us aboard tonight, but we shall have to hide until we can blend with the large crowd in the morn," Olivia said. "We are unauthorized passengers, my daughter. I ought to have explained everything better beforehand. Mr. Chandler also made arrangements for Constance to travel in secret."

The wagon driver returned. His beady eyes peered out of a face mostly covered in hair, and he reeked of alcohol. After a moment, he bent down and threw the trunk over a broad shoulder.

"Follow me and remaineth close," he uttered in a slur.

Sybil stepped on the wood slats and wrinkled her nose at the strong smell of fish and seawater. Beneath nets, several stacked crates, barrels, and chests flanked her as she moved down the pier. Against the cold starry sky, she gazed up at the ship masts where many sails had been rolled up amid a crisscrossing network of ropes and pulleys. She never imagined sailing on such a vessel, let alone traveling across the ocean for several weeks.

She suddenly realized her mother had lagged behind to speak with the other burly man. Sybil stopped and heard them arguing in the glow of an oil lamp resting on a crate.

"Where is the rest of the payment owed?" the man demanded.

"I have given forth the proper amount we agreed upon," Olivia responded. "There is more than enough to compensate for your trouble."

"Trouble? Look you, I run these docks and have a trustworthy reputation for documenting every flea and hair aboard these ships. Do you conceive what would happen if the captain discovered I snuck passengers onto his vessel? Thereof I would end up in leg irons! And worse, soon I shall have witch-hunters upon me. That is a lot more trouble than I need, thus the rate has increased. Forthwith halt your prattle and give me my money!"

Olivia shifted her feet and fidgeted with the cuff of her sleeve. "That is all I possess, good sir. Please, take it and allow me to board with my daughter. The other young woman, Constance Chandler, hath she arrived?"

"She is already onboard." The man bounced a sack of coins in a hand before placing the money in a pocket. "There is enough for your daughter, but not for you." He reached into his coat, and Sybil gasped when he withdrew a knife. "The payment," he growled. "I shall not ask again."

Olivia shuffled back. "I beg you, please let me pass. I already gave forth more than enough."

The man stepped toward her. "It matters not that you are witches, I warrant your coin is just as good as anyone's. But since you have no more, I fancy I shall take a different form of payment." He slid an arm around Olivia's waist and buried his face in her neck.

"Mother!" Sybil cried in panic. She darted forward, but the man holding the trunk dropped it to the boards and grabbed her upper arm. The dress tore at the shoulder as he threw her down and pinned her body using a large boot.

Olivia and the other large brute struggled for a moment before a bright flash erupted from her fingers. The man shouted in pain and pressed a hand against a sudden burn on the side of his face. She turned to run, but the attacker grabbed the back of her dress. His other arm flew over the top of Olivia's shoulder and slammed the knife into her chest.

Shock numbed Sybil, and she froze. A sharp ringing blared in her ears. Disbelief severed her mind from the world. Only a dream. Yes…everything had happened so fast tonight this couldn't be real. Even the hard boot grinding her into the damp boards didn't mean anything. She would wake in her bed at any moment.

Out of nowhere, a young woman ran past and toward Olivia's prone body on the dock. The pressure on Sybil's back eased as the man removed his foot to chase after the girl. Catching her in a few long strides, the bearded crewmember spun the woman around and struck her across the face. Sybil now recognized Constance Chandler as she fell, unconscious.

Reality crashed over Sybil in a discord of pain and misery. Ears still ringing, she rose on weak legs and stumbled toward her mother. In the oil lamp's glow, Olivia's eyes stared at nothing as blood pooled beneath her. Sybil's mouth flew open, her horrified scream locked in a perpetual howl. Nausea threatened to empty her stomach on the wharf. Somehow heating on its own, the pentacle on the necklace grew warm against her chest, but an attempt at magic failed her. Confusion shattered her mind in darkness. Her body seemed to float in a void, useless and unresponsive.

A strong hand clamped over Sybil's mouth and another gripped her upper arm. She cried against a large sweaty palm, her vision blurred by tears.

"You fool!" the bearded man shouted at the assassin. "Enough problems ail us. What shall we do forthwith?"

The murderer put the weapon away and scooped up Olivia's body. He walked to the wagon and placed Sybil's mother inside. Seeing the bottle of alcohol on the seat, he brought it to his lips and finished the contents in several large gulps.

"Fear not, I shall remedy the situation," he uttered in a hoarse voice. "Get those girls on yonder ship. They have nowhere else to go and shall not say a word lest the witch-hunters lay eyes on them."

The bearded man uncovered Sybil's mouth and continued his hold on her arm. "Mother!" she screamed again.

She struggled in his grip, feet skidding as she fought to reach Olivia. The man's sharp blow to the side of Sybil's head dropped her to the boards in a daze. He pulled her up and yanked her toward Constance, who had stirred at some point and swayed on her knees. The pitiless man grabbed Constance by the neck of her dress and hauled both girls further down the pier towards the *John of London*.

After crossing over the wooden gangplank, the dockhand threw the girls down on the main deck. Sybil tried to stand, but a sharp kick to her midsection left her stunned. The man returned a short time later with her trunk.

"It would behoove you to stay onboard and keep your mouths shut," he said wafting a foul, alcohol-laced breath. "I might summon the witch-hunters to the docks just to make sure you remaineth hidden. After you are across yonder ocean, I shall never have to worry about either of you again." He departed the vessel, his feet pounding the boards in a sprint down the wharf.

Pressing a hand over her throbbing midsection, Sybil dragged herself to the edge of the ship. Dizzy and short of breath, she strained to rise on feeble legs. Leaning against the wooden railing, she finally peered across Plymouth harbor.

The men and the wagon carrying her mother were gone.

Hard sobs shook Sybil as she collapsed on the deck. Intense, emotional pain bored through her chest. Anguish twisted her mind in chaos, and she found it difficult to breathe. She suddenly desired to throw herself into the sea, if only to escape the torment.

Warm, soft arms slid around her from behind. A sweet, low voice sang a lullaby in her ear. The arms rocked Sybil in a gentle rhythm, and she melted back into a momentary bliss of escape. The melody ignited childhood memories of innocent, happier times with her family. Cozy fires and roasted nuts, holiday meals, a snug bed while dozing between her mother and father.

The final notes ended, and Sybil opened her eyes. Feeling somewhat calm, the night's horror resided in a distant corner of her mind instead of dominating all thought and emotion. She gazed down at the protective arms still holding her, then turned in the grasp to meet Constance's battered face and disheveled blond curls in the moonlight. The young woman's right eye had nearly swollen shut from the blow, and dried blood caked her nostrils.

"How do you fare, darling?" Constance asked, managing a smile.

"I am better. 'Twas much more than just a lullaby, I warrant?"

Constance nodded. "Truly, I laced enchanted words into the song to put you at ease." Sorrow then lowered her gaze as tears ran down her cheeks. "I already stood hither on the ship when I heard the commotion on yonder docks. I am sorry I could not strive more to help your mother. Of a truth, my abilities are rather limited."

As the ship bobbed on the water, the deck swayed in a steady pace and reminded Sybil of how Constance had rocked her like a baby. She lifted a hand and carefully stroked the side of the young woman's face. "Truly, you did more than enough, Constance. Now I shall help you in return. I have a sundry of healing herbs in my trunk."

Working through fresh tears and flashes of nightmare, Sybil's trembling hands prepared a remedy made from rosemary and thyme soaked in lavender oil. Both girls seated on the chest, she gently dabbed the poultice on Constance's face and around her eye.

"Where are your parents?" Sybil asked. "Shall they be joining us on the morrow?"

At the inquiry, she could tell Constance did her best not to cry as she shook her head. "My mother is close to giving birth, thus my father cannot leave her side," Constance began. "I am nineteen years of age, and my father decided he would do everything to get me safely out of Plymouth on my own. They shall join me in yonder Colonies as soon as possible."

It sounded like Constance recited a difficult conversation she had had with her parents. Sybil took the young woman into her arms. "You shall see them again and with a new little brother or sister to spoil." She pulled back and smiled softly. "Your family shall have a better life in the New World. All of this shall just be a distant memory…for the both of us." Sybil gritted her teeth and fought off a swoon. Not even able to conduct a burial, the vision of her dead mother being hoisted into the wagon tore her heart wider after each painful beat.

Constance's gentle touch steadied Sybil. "You must dwell with my family," the young woman offered. "I would not have it any other way."

"That sounds wonderful, I warrant," Sybil said, trying to push the darkness from her mind. "Aunt Sybil would love to take care of your new sibling."

Voices on the dock caused her heart to jump. She gazed down the wharf and spotted several lamps and shadowy figures moving across the boards.

"Get down!" she whispered in panic.

The girls flattened themselves on the upper deck. Not daring to move, Sybil closed her eyes and listened as the voices grew louder. Was it the witch-hunters, the night watch, or other dock workers? If any one of those groups, her journey would end the moment she and Constance were spotted.

An eternity passed. Sybil lay rigid and tense until the voices finally faded. She dared to peer over the top rail and saw the lamps moving farther away.

"Let us settle below the deck," she said quietly. "Sunrise shall be here soon, and we need to rest as much as possible."

They wrestled their belongings down some steps and saw an old hammock to lay in. The girls held each other and found warmth against the cold, yet the pressing darkness and the eerie groan of wood did nothing to improve Sybil's mood. But for the moment, she felt content to have Constance at her side.

"On the morrow, we shall begin our voyage," Sybil stated, nestling against her friend. "And of a truth, I shall not be looking back."

***

Three weeks into the sea, Sybil caught a terrible illness. Drenched in sweat, she lay on the hammock and shivered as the rough sway of the ship added to her misery. Light and darkness swam before her half-lidded eyes. Days and nights passed in mad fever-dreams and nightmares. Not the only one ill, other passengers around her coughed, moaned, and cried in unending torment during a cruel voyage of vast discomfort, stench, and slow progress.

Sybil had few moments of lucidity, and during those times, she grew aware of Constance working herself into the grave just to take care of her. The young woman had said her abilities were limited, but that didn't stop her from having the love, courage, and resolve to keep Sybil from dying.

Constance never stopped her treatments. Weak and unable to move, Sybil fought to remain conscious while bits of food and water were placed into her mouth. Sometimes an herbal remedy slipped between her lips, and the medicine lay bitter on her tongue. On these occasions, Constance whispered incantations, and Sybil realized her dear friend risked exposure as a witch in order to defeat the illness.

During the most arduous nights, Sybil dreamed of faeries and tree spirits singing to her in the woods as peace bathed her in splendor. She would then wake and discover Constance singing softly at her side, dabbing Sybil's body with a moist cloth.

One morning, she opened her eyes and saw her friend's pale, haggard face while she changed Sybil's clothes. Dark half-moons floated beneath Constance's eyes, and she looked like death as apparently the illness overcame her as well. Sybil tried to speak, to tell the young woman to rest and take care of herself, but communication eluded her. She then tried to gesture, but her arm felt as if weighed by iron. Apprehension over Constance's health plagued Sybil as she fell into blackness once again.

An indefinite time later, the fever broke. Sybil woke groggy, but also feeling as if a gigantic weight had been lifted from her body. Daylight filtered into the crowded sleep chamber below the main deck as the vessel moved in a gentle rhythm. She glanced around and saw several passengers lounging in hammocks, speaking among themselves, or rummaging through their belongings. Above, a crewman shouted orders to other deckhands.

Sybil swung her legs over the edge of the hammock and paused until a wave of dizziness passed. Hunger gnawed her insides, a good sign of recovery as much needed nourishment would return more of her strength. Standing, her eyes fell on Constance sprawled asleep on the hard boards with rumpled clothing piled beneath her head as a pillow. Her mouth hung open, face exhausted and glowing in a sheen of sweat.

A powerful wave of admiration and love burst inside Sybil as she gazed upon her companion. The dedication and sacrifice Constance had shown during Sybil's illness, as well as her own, proved beyond extraordinary. Throughout the long voyage, the young woman had been Sybil's sister, mother, and best friend. She had represented home, memory, and warmth of heart. Just as Sybil had vowed not to be a burden to her mother, she now promised the same for Constance. The girl had done so much already, and Sybil desired to protect her friend and return the same level of care, if not more.

She prepared a batch of medicine while careful to avoid any unwanted attention. She combined some catswort, clove, and elderflower to aide in reducing fever. She then shoved the tightly rolled mass inside a piece of bread, and woke her friend.

"Eat, my dear," she said.

Using a bit of water, Constance slowly ingested the remedy. She gazed up at Sybil, concern in her hazel eyes.

"I am faring well," Sybil announced. "You rest forthwith and allow me to take care of you."

Unable to lift Constance into the hammock, Sybil settled on the floor and wrapped her arms around her friend. Both girls slept peacefully, and together they made a full recovery over the next two days.

A few weeks later, the *John of London* arrived in the city of Boston.

Chapter Two

Salem Village, Massachusetts 1692

"Spirits of soil and rulers of earth, come forth like flame dancing in a hearth. Beneath the Maiden moon her will we must know, to bring life and desire for these crops to grow!"

In the darkness of night, Sybil finished the incantation while standing in a rye field outside the village. A sliver of waxing moon cut into the sky like a scythe, similar to what the farmers would do to the crop provided she could spur a healthy growth. The entire community had struggled with food this season, so Sybil took action through spellcraft—in secret, of course—to try and put food in people's bellies.

Three years had passed since she departed England. She had traveled to Salem Village and settled there with Constance in a small cottage. Fear and hatred of witches followed the colonists to the New World, but Sybil had not been naïve enough to truly believe her problems ended once the ship arrived in Boston. Sybil, Constance, and other witches they had met continued to practice their craft in private, away from the citizens' religious fervor and paranoia. Life here had been difficult, full of hard toil, and worst of all filled with a constant fear for their wellbeing. But surpassing all, the love and friendship between Sybil and Constance had only grown stronger and made the two young women inseparable.

Sybil gazed around the shadowy rye field while holding a jar. The water inside had been charged with light from the waxing moon. The Maiden of the Triple Moon Goddess governed this phase of the celestial body, and it represented a time of beginnings, initiation, enhancement, and growth—hopefully for these stubborn crops.

She moved slowly around the large field while sprinkling the enchanted water throughout the area. After finishing with the rye, she strolled to the pumpkin patch to repeat the incantations and dash the water over the harvest. Afterwards, she met up with Constance after her friend had performed the same spell for the squash and beans.

"That is the last of it," Constance said in a low voice as they ducked behind a haystack near a horse pasture. "The rest is up to yonder Maiden. The hour is very late. Shall we go home?"

"Of a truth, I still need to treat Mr. Dowling's joint aches," Sybil replied. "I shall meet you at the cottage."

Constance sighed. "Fear overcomes me every time you help someone in the village. Several weeks agone and hitherto, the constable, the magistrates, and other town officials have been scrutinizing several people more and more. They accused Bridget Bishop of witchcraft, and her trial is on the morrow! Truly, one day they might put you on the stand, too."

Sybil squeezed her friend's hand. "I am careful about who I converse with, I warrant. Most of Salem would expose us without hesitation, but that shall not stop me from curing ailments for ungrateful patients or healing crops without anyone perceiving of it. Everyone hath experienced a difficult life in the Colonies, and it is the least I can do."

Constance leaned forward and kissed Sybil's forehead. "You brave, foolish girl. Come home quickly, and I shall have something prepared to eat."

Sybil watched her friend depart. Over the past three years, Constance had not received a single letter by ship or word about her family from new arrivals. Sybil had accompanied her to the port every time a vessel docked, then watched in sorrow as Constance observed the disembarking passengers and repeatedly failed to find her family. The woman never cried or complained; she would only give a small nod to the sea as if to say, *next time*. On those days Sybil tried to console her, but Constance did her best to show strength and continue her routine of cooking, cleaning, and spell-work with nothing to say. It was Sybil who went outside to weep in private for Constance while sharing her friend's silent anguish.

"I shall be home soon, my dear beloved," Sybil whispered in the starlit gloom.

***

The next morning, a heavy stillness floated through the streets of Salem Village as officials, residents, and trial participants packed the town hall. Most of the businesses remained closed, but Sybil had been fortunate with her purchase of sewing supplies so she could mend a few dresses. Unnerved by the trial, she hurried home and exchanged an anxious look with Constance. Hoping for Bridget's acquittal, both girls worked in their own tense hush while completing chores.

Sometime later, a dull roar from the town center halted the broom in Sybil's hands. She met Constance's wide-eyed gaze, and they immediately left their tasks to join a raucous crowd milling through the street.

Sybil's heart thundered as she followed the throng outside the village and into a sloped meadow. What was this about? Where was Bridget? Reaching a cluster of trees, Sybil clamped a hand over her mouth to stop a terrified shriek. Shock weakened her knees as tears fell.

Perched on a ladder, Bridget's aghast, white face stood above the crowd. Ropes bound her hands behind her back. Secured to a tree branch, a noose dangled, the loop tightened around her neck.

"This cannot be," Sybil uttered, her voice drowned out by the boisterous mob.

The hangman kicked the ladder, and a horrific jolt choked the life out of Bridget Bishop. Her body swung from the branch, the noose tight and unyielding, a crude tool for killing innocent and defenseless women accused of witchcraft.

Disgusted, enraged, and sick with grief, Sybil stood rigid among the stunned and elated spectators. Some people cried while others gasped, their eyes wide and mouths agape in pallid faces. Other citizens cheered and nodded in satisfaction; these paranoid, ignorant, and heartless people believed the witch trial and execution would end their troubles of failed crops, illness, and food shortages in the Colonies.

Sybil wiped her tears and turned away from the gruesome scene. The crowd dispersed amid murmurs and swishing feet down the elevated grassy acres outside of town. A hand grabbed her upper arm, and she nearly screamed. She turned and met Constance's panicked face.

"Sybil, we could be next," Constance whispered in a trembling voice. "I am so frightened!"

"Shh! We shall speak elsewhere." Sybil led her distraught friend down the grassy incline and through the meadow until they reached the village. The warm, midday sun failed to bring a hint of joy on this terrible day in June. Sybil realized that Bridget's death would not be the last. If she wasn't careful, Constance's prediction might prove true.

Holding hands, Sybil dodged a knot of clomping horses and continued past a string of shops until reaching the large group of wooden, thatch-roofed homes. She entered their residence and locked the door, then pulled all the curtains shut. After lighting a fire, she hung a pot over the flames to make tea.

Constance would not sit down. She yanked off her white coif and revealed curly, shoulder-length blond hair. Pacing the parlor, the wool skirt beneath her buttoned waistcoat rustled around her ankles. She used a handkerchief to dry fresh tears from her eyes. "Bridget was not even a witch. These trials are going to kill more innocent girls, I warrant. What shall we do, Sybil? We shall run away again…yes, forthwith. Let us go far away from this place."

Sybil threw some tea leaves into the simmering pot, then reached into the front of her waistcoat to take out the necklace with the silver pentacle. She recalled the terrible night when her mother had gifted her the jewelry and later lost her life in a brutal murder.

Constance's mouth dropped open. "Put that away forthwith! Do you want the whole town to smash in the door and drag us to yonder tree?"

Sybil held the necklace in a firm grip. She also held tight to her resolve for justice. After witnessing Bridget suffer, Sybil swore no more women would hang for crimes they didn't commit. "Constance, poor Bridget died because of what you and I represent. We are real witches, but Salem's calamities have nothing to do with our craft. Of a truth, I have been running away my entire life and forthwith I refuse to. I shall testify in court and explain to the officials what is truly happening. Someone must halt this madness before it gets worse."

Constance touched the dangling pentacle. "You have always been so courageous, Sybil. I would not conceive what to do without you, I warrant. In England, our parents sacrificed everything to secure us safe passage to the Colonies so we could escape the witch hunts. But hitherto in Salem Village, the paranoia and witch hunting have started anew. I also do believe something must be done to stop this, but the situation remaineth too dangerous."

Sybil placed the necklace back inside her coat. Her family had been persecuted for generations. Would the violence ever stop? How long would she have to live in fear? So much sadness and pain, for her and other witches who had lost everything.

"Are you well?" Constance asked. "You look as though you wish to burn down the world."

Sybil blinked out of her reverie, and the blood drained from her heated face. The memory of her mother's sacrifice still brought nightmares, sorrow, and rage. People were so ignorant of witchcraft's history and capabilities. Throughout the centuries, society's naivety and fear of the unknown had destroyed numerous lives. Only eighteen, Sybil had already experienced a lifetime of discrimination and needing to perform her craft in secret.

"I fare well." Sybil stepped to the boiling pot and removed it from the fire. Placing two cups on the table, she poured the tea and set out two spoons alongside a small jar of honey. "I was thinking of my mother."

Constance moved to Sybil, and the young women slipped arms around each other in a warm hug. "We have dwelled in this cottage for three years," said Constance. "I am twenty-two years of age, yet I warrant you are the one looking after me." She leaned back and smiled. "You are like my mother, even making my favorite tea."

Sybil slipped her fingers through her friend's beautiful, natural curls. "Although it is only both of us, Constance, we are a coven. I was so frightened when we left England years agone, but I found strength having you at my side. We have striven to create a life for ourselves, and I know we shall overcome these difficult times."

A hard pound on the door rattled its hinges. Sybil's heart jumped, and she exchanged a terrified look with Constance.

"Sybil Radella Cotterill, this is the constable. Open the door forthwith!"

"No!" Constance uttered in a panicked whisper. "They have come to take you away."

"I think not," Sybil replied calmly, although her heart continued to hammer like the fist on the door. "Truly, if charges stood against me, yonder men would force their way inside. Remaineth hither and try to compose yourself. I shall return as soon as I can."

Sybil had to pry her arm from Constance's frantic grab. With sweat moistening her palms and prickling her lower back, she opened the door to a knot of grim-faced men standing in the shade of her porch. She recognized the constable, Daniel. "Greetings, Constable. There hath been enough drama for today. How may I be of service?"

Daniel's buttoned doublet appeared too small for his bulging stomach. The stockings pulled up to his knees were torn, and dirt stained his breeches. Sweat coated his reddened face; clearly the constable had been busy during and after Bridget's execution. "Miss Cotterill, your presence is required in yonder town hall at once. Some governing officials shall speak with you."

"Of course. I actually desire to speak with the officials as well." Sybil stepped outside and closed the door behind her. Ironically, she had just stated her intentions to try and placate the court over the witch hysteria. However, why had Daniel brought so many men with him? Why hadn't the summons included Constance as well?

The men surrounded her as she strolled through the dirt street toward the town hall. Most of the citizens had returned to their routines by now, and many of them halted to stare. On the wooden porch of his leather shop, a man's broom paused in mid-stroke. A pair of chatting women on a bench stopped fanning their faces. A bare-chested fellow hesitated while repairing a horse carriage.

Sybil swallowed and took a deep breath when entering the building used for municipal and judicial purposes. The men's heavy steps and her light ones echoed on the wooden planks of the lobby. A large stone fireplace sat in the far wall where two sofas flanked a bearskin rug. The men stopped at a reception desk while a woman scratched in a ledger using a quill.

Sybil took a moment to look at her haggard reflection in a wide mirror over the hearth. Wisps of her light brown hair escaped the coif along the sides of her face and brow. The barest of freckles clustered high on her cheeks beneath light brown eyes. *You have eyes the color of afternoon tea, and hair the color of fresh baked biscuits*, her mother used to say.

"Make haste," Daniel's voice boomed.

The men had finished checking in. Sybil left the group and continued with the constable as he escorted her down a short hallway.

Within a spacious office, several magistrates sat stiff in chairs. All eyes pierced Sybil as she entered and found herself the center of attention. Her breath caught when she spotted Minister Kendrick, the head of the church, standing in the back of the room. The afternoon sunlight spilled through the windows, yet an uncanny shadow seemed to drape over Kendrick. The flesh on his darkened face resembled the wrinkled bark of a tree. The copper-skinned, black-haired old man had no pupils or irises. Instead, a sickening yellow the color of phlegm filled his eye sockets. No one knew if he was blind; no one dared ask, although the man never faltered as he moved about.

A year ago, Minister Kendrick arrived in Salem Village from England, but Sybil doubted the man had English roots due to his strange accent. Since arriving, Kendrick quickly established himself as the town's church leader. He also inserted himself into the community's politics and never left Chief Justice Stoughton's side. Rumors stated the minister always whispered in the Chief Justice's ear, pulled him aside during meetings, or had Stoughton sign mysterious documents. When the Chief Justice pounded his gavel and sent Bridget Bishop to the gallows, Kendrick had surely been there.

Along with the minister's horrid appearance and his enigmatic activities around Salem, Kendrick's presence in the office signified a grave occasion. Goosebumps rose on Sybil's arms, and she shuddered.

"Wherefore are you all assembled?" she asked the group. "Is this event a trial? Where is Chief Justice Stoughton?"

"Have some respect, Miss Cotterill," Daniel demanded. "They shall ask the questions, not you."

"This occasion is not a trial, young Sybil, only an informal inquiry," one of the magistrates said. "And the Chief Justice's whereabouts are none of your concern." The man turned in his chair to glance at Kendrick, and the minister gave a slight nod.

The magistrate faced Sybil again. "My name is Barton Acker, and I shall ask you some questions."

"If it would please you to tell me why I am—"

"Silence! As you conceive, Miss Cotterill, Salem Village hath been plagued by very dangerous events as of late. Children are suffering fits, crops are dying, and people are falling ill. Witches are at work in our town, I warrant. Our duty is to protect the citizens, thus my fellow magistrates and I have commenced a series of investigations."

"Your inquiries led to an innocent woman's death!" Sybil pronounced in a loud voice. Unable to maintain control, her anger and frustration surged as she threw a tirade at the seated members. "Of a truth, Bridget never hurt anyone and witches did not cause the town's problems. Hitherto, the citizens are fearful over King William's war with New France in the Colonies. The smallpox epidemic hath also unsettled everyone.

"Mr. Acker, all of us left England and sailed hither to the strange New World. Dwelling on the edge of civilization, we risk death by starvation and exposure while surrounded by wilderness and angry native tribes. Truly, our situation creates high levels of tension, and people fancy any excuse to blame their fears on. Thereof, failed crops and wild imaginations do not mean witches are poisoning the land or casting curses."

"Are you finished, Miss Cotterill?" Barton asked. "'Twas an admirable speech, but facts are facts. The devil remaineth at work in Salem, and that means lies and deceit. Answer this question forthwith. Three years agone, you and Constance Chandler arrived in Massachusetts aboard the vessel *John of London*, is that correct?"

"You speak true, but wherein does that have to do with all this?"

Barton slipped a hand into his waistcoat and produced a worn document. "This is the shipping manifest from the *John of London*, signed by the vessel's master, George Lamberton. Every sundry of cargo and passenger is listed. Every single person on the manifest hath been accounted for, except for you and Constance."

Sybil's throat went dry. "Mr. Acker, I feel certain there is a reasonable—"

"Your names are not recorded here," Barton continued. "I know George, and of a truth, he would never commit an error like this on his ship. When names are absent from a document such as this, it means someone hath striven to hide something."

"Mr. Acker, I do not conceive anything about shipping lists," Sybil responded. "I was only fifteen years of age that time agone. Uneducated, poor, and thrown onto a ship with dozens of strangers. Of a truth, I could have never tampered with such a thing. I would not know how and had no reason to."

"I conceive that, which is why you are not the main suspect," said Barton.

"What do you speak of?" Sybil asked in alarm. Her mother had made the arrangements for passage, but she was no longer here.

"How well do you know Constance Chandler?" Barton asked, ignoring Sybil's question.

"We became good friends after arriving in Salem Village and decided to dwell together," she answered. "I know her quite well. Truly, aforesaid this is not a trial, so I shall return home." She turned and stepped to the door, but Daniel blocked the way.

"Just a few more questions," said Barton.

Sybil scrutinized the gathered magistrates. A few of them leaned toward each other and whispered behind their hands. Others wrote notes, their severe faces holding no sympathy. Minister Kendrick had not moved at all. He stood rigid and imposing, his blank eyes prominent in the shadows smothering the back of the office.

"I have received disquieting reports about your home," Barton began. "During the last two full moons, glass jars filled with water sat on your back patio. On one of these late nights, someone had a fair sight of Constance roaming the trees on your property. A candle was also found there. Explain forthwith."

Heat flared on Sybil's cheeks as her temper quelled the fear. How long had the magistrates been spying on her home? Were all the women in town being watched like this? She had been lucky no one had seen her and Constance in the crop fields last night. The notion of being caught sickened her. Vulnerable, restless, and apprehensive, she had to escape this situation fast…and act confident and careful with her words while doing so.

"'Twas some time agone, thus forgive me if I do not recall every small detail," said Sybil.

She actually remembered those nights very well. The light of a full moon contained intense magical properties. The celestial rays had charged the water in the jars to be used as a base for various spells, just as the waxing moon had done for the harvest. As for Constance being outside, she had gone into the trees to invoke a sprite so the creature could bless the candle with natural healing energy.

"I believe the jars had been filled from the well…cooking water that was probably forgotten and left outside," Sybil began. "Truly, I do not know one day from the next, so this occurring on two consecutive full moons was just coincidence. Constance more than likely used the privy outside with a candle to light the way.

Thereof, I do not think these activities are odd. What I do find strange is being spied upon in the middle of yonder night. Forthwith, I really am going to leave."

She turned and faced Daniel. "Constable, unless I am being arrested for hiding on a ship three years agone, you shall please step aside."

Daniel ignored the magistrates and looked only at Minister Kendrick. The old man gave a slight nod again, and Daniel moved away from the door.

Sybil left the office and paused when she reached the lobby. The group of men who had arrived with her earlier had left. She should have been relieved the uninvited escort wouldn't follow her home, yet intuition made her uneasy over the men's absence.

"Miss, I need you to sign for your appearance forthwith," the woman at the reception desk called.

Disregarding the request, Sybil hiked up her skirts and ran out of the building. Her agitation worsened as she sprinted down the street. Something felt wrong. If the magistrates hadn't called her in to accuse her of something, then why…

I conceive that, which is why you are not the main suspect. Barton's words had suddenly blared in Sybil's head.

"'Twas not me they were after," she said to herself, out of breath. "No…Constance!"

Sybil dashed onto her property. All hope vanished when she saw the broken front door. She charged into the house and discovered a chaotic mess. In the kitchen, the table lay overturned and chairs rested on their sides. Cooking utensils, containers, and food littered the floor. In the living room, desk drawers had been pulled out, their contents dumped on the rug. In the bedroom, the beds had been flipped over and the bureau emptied of clothes and shoes.

"Constance, where are you?" she shouted.

Sybil nearly fainted when she found a specific floorboard ripped up in the farthest corner. The hidden compartment beneath the wood sat empty. Her spell tome was gone, along with her friend.

She ran outside and found several residents hurrying beyond the town limits, in the direction of the execution site on the hill. Excited and dread-filled conversation rippled through the crowd. Sybil raced past the citizens and up the grassy slope. She reached a mob gathered before the large tree where Bridget had been killed only a few hours earlier.

Hands bound behind her back, Constance stood halfway up a ladder, a noose around her neck. Shock froze her pallid face, hazel eyes wide and mouth slightly ajar.

"Stop!" Sybil screamed. "You cannot do this. There hath not been a trial. Where is Chief Justice Stoughton?"

"Mr. Stoughton hath given me all authority in this matter," a voice called from behind the throng.

Falling silent, the crowd parted to allow Minister Kendrick through as he strolled to the tree dressed in a black robe. His gangly frame stopped at the summit as bare, lifeless eyes bored into Sybil. His dry, wrinkled copper skin seemed to wither under the sun. A mild breeze tousled the thick black hair on his head.

"These actions are illegal, Minister Kendrick," Sybil stated, trembling in panic. "Release Constance at once!"

"Truly, all of the legal documentation is signed on my desk," said Kendrick. "The Chief Justice and his magistrates have been very understanding hitherto. Constance Chandler is accused of carrying out the devil's work through witchcraft. She shall hang for her crimes."

"You have no proof," Sybil countered, although she knew the minister did.

Kendrick reached into his robe and revealed Sybil's spell tome. He raised it and the crowd gasped. "Crop poisoning, animal mutilation, triggering fits, curses of disease…it is all written here. Salem shall not stand for this. All witches shall be purged from the Colonies."

"Yonder book is mine, and no such spells reside in it!" Sybil pleaded. Sweat moistened her skin, and nausea roiled in her stomach as she faced the riled mob. "Minister Kendrick is lying. He hath manipulated this town for years. Please, allow me to explain forthwith. I have striven to help this town with my magic—"

A stone flew from the gathering and struck above her right eye. She crashed to the ground, dazed. Blood trickled down her face and dripped onto the grass.

"She hath admitted to being a witch!" the stone-thrower yelled. The people roared their condemnation and chanted for Sybil's death.

Minister Kendrick turned to Daniel and the group of men that had escorted Sybil to the town hall. "String her up next to her blasphemous friend."

Rough hands seized Sybil as the men tied her hands behind her. They pushed her up the steps of a second ladder someone placed next to Constance. Another rope flew over the thick branch. The abrasive noose slid around her neck, and the running knot tightened behind her right ear. The horde's curses and chants grew louder.

Weak, dizzy, and bloodied, her head throbbed as she battled a swoon. Breathing heavily, she glanced over to her beloved friend. The confused and terrified young woman had not moved.

"Sweetheart," Sybil called in an unsteady voice. "You must fight forthwith. There is no hiding anymore. Use your abilities, I know you can do it." Constance remained still. "Look at me!"

Slowly, Constance rotated her head until she stared, but no life or emotion filled her eyes. Sybil saw someone beyond reach, lost in darkness and surrounded by deep waters with no end. Petrified, Constance's world had shattered around her. She no longer realized her whereabouts. Yet her lips formed a small smile, a sign of affection Sybil would never forget.

Her distraught mind reached out for magic…and found nothing. It was the same as her mother once again. Sybil had failed to intervene on the docks that day, and now her effort to save Constance arrived too late.

The hangman kicked the ladder away, and Constance jerked on the rope. Sybil's wail drowned out the cheering mob. The force of her scream nearly ruptured her throat as emotional pain tore out her heart. She thrashed in her bindings and the ropes cut her skin. Sweat poured over her body. Through teary eyes, she met Minister Kendrick's gaze and found no amusement or satisfaction. Only intense concentration showed as if the wicked man anticipated something.

On the talisman tucked inside Sybil's waistcoat, the bottom-left point of the pentagram began to glow red with heat until it branded the skin above her breasts.

Earth.

The ground below her shook as she somehow cast a spell. Cracks tore the hilltop, and rolling waves of soil piled beneath her. The hangman managed to kick the ladder. Sybil plummeted…then landed on the mound of dirt, the noose slack around her neck.

Where had this newfound ability come from? She had never been capable of such a powerful display of magic. She could barely get the village's crops to recover. Her extensive training as a child allowed her to manipulate the elements, but on a much lower scale. She recalled the pentacle warming when her mother had been killed—why hadn't she been able to exploit the magic then?

The bottom-right point of the pentagram heated against her chest, searing her flesh.

Fire.

The ropes binding her wrists ignited in flame. The twine snapped and fell away. Arms free and unburned by her magic, she worked the noose off her neck and stepped down from the knoll as the crowd fled in terror.

Sybil perceived no life remaining in her dearest friend. A single tear coursed down her cheek, though it held no emotion. She felt nothing, *was* nothing. Her heart beat, but she did not live. She breathed, yet did not exist. A dull, rusted instrument had scraped her insides and left a cold hollow. Pain and intense grief floated deep in her subconscious, the last remnants of her humanity as a thirst for revenge exploded inside.

Sybil looked for Kendrick, but the man had vanished. She ran down the path in the wake of screaming citizens. Reaching the town square, she lifted a hand and a small flame danced on her palm. She cast the fire toward a wagon, and the flame ignited a pile of burlap sacks.

Another point on the pentagram, the top-left, pressed a red-hot scar into her chest.

Air.

A strong wind roared through the square to fan the flames. Tendrils of fire lifted from the burning wagon. The blazing wisps sailed overhead and landed on rooftops. Smoke curled into the sky as wooden stores and several homes turned into crackling, smoking infernos.

Sybil neared the stone well and used the bucket to draw water. She wet her hand and flicked drops of moisture into the air. On the pentacle dangling around her neck, the top-right point of the star glowed, its color and heat like the fire consuming the town.

Water.

She took a deep breath and called out. "*Water of life, boiled by strife, my vengeance burns in fire. Drops glisten, the spirits listen, a black curse my desire!*"

The topmost and final point on the pentagram burned—*Spirit.*

Sybil continued her spell. "*The divine I implore, from my heart evermore, the deities know my mind. Quick as a lark, let the ash leave its mark, for these murderers I shall find!*"

A knot of wood exploded on the blazing wagon. Dozens of fiery embers roared into the sky. Like fireflies, the cherry-red embers sailed in various directions in pursuit of the mob involved in Constance's death. Running panicked through the burning streets of Salem Village, the magistrates, the constable, his cronies, and the cruel witnesses at the tree would not escape the cinders. The flying embers cooled into ash and stained the back of people's hands to mark them for life. Powered by her spell, the black marks served as beacons that would allow Sybil an easy hunt of her victims.

"Run, you heartless cowards," she whispered. "It matters not where you go or what you do. I shall find you."

"Very impressive," a voice said behind her.

Sybil whirled and froze. Minister Kendrick stood in the street, a small smile beneath his yellowed eyes. Weakened by fire, the porch of a nearby cobbler shop buckled in a roar of flame. The man had not fled, and the blazing town didn't seem to bother him.

Before Sybil could react, Kendrick gestured, and her body stiffened. An unseen force squeezed her tight. Her tongue and throat swelled. She could barely breathe, let alone speak. How could this be? She never imagined the minister possessed mystical powers. And this strange force—she had never encountered anything like it before. Who, or what, was Kendrick really?

For the first time that day, Sybil's rage faded and true fear welled inside her.

Kendrick moved close, his horrid gaze washing over her. He licked the blackened ash on the back of his hand, and the mark disappeared, nullifying her magic on him. His crumpled face then beamed in excitement. "This is wonderful, Miss Cotterill! Of a truth, it took me nine countries and over a hundred years to finally find what I need. From my origins in the Inca Empire to yonder shores of Europe and back to the New World, I have searched for a witch such as you."

He gazed around the fiery, ruined street. Intense heat from the burning buildings made him sweat. "Such an amazing display of witchcraft, I warrant. The timing of your age with the trauma you experienced were the keys to unlocking your true potential. Thereof, you are still not ready. I conceive much more power within you."

Constance…

Sybil's trepidation slowly melted into a deep, penetrating sorrow. Unable to move or speak, silent tears poured from her eyes as she thought of her friend.

"Do not be troubled, young one," said Kendrick. "Forthwith you shall sleep for over three centuries, and all this shall be but a distant memory. During your slumber, your abilities shall grow even more potent. Like a fine wine, your body and spirit need time in the cellar to reach their best."

The minister spoke nonsense. Sybil had no idea what the deranged man had in mind, but if she had to endure a sleep of that duration, then ample time remained to dream of vengeance.

Kendrick reached into her waistcoat and ripped out the pentacle. Holding the chain in a gnarled grip, he inspected the encircled star. The metal appeared cool after her spell casting. "Worry not, Miss Cotterill, I just need to borrow this for a while. It shall be returned to you along with your spell tome."

Mumbling strange words, Kendrick brushed the back of his fingers across Sybil's forehead. Helpless, dejected, and bitter with fury, she closed her eyes and remembered nothing more.

Chapter Three

San Luis Obispo, California - Present Day

"Ladies and gentlemen, before we commence the SLO Jazz Festival, I would like to honor our sponsor and very special guest, Marcelo Abana Flores," the emcee announced into the microphone. "Mr. Flores, please come to the stage."

To a round of applause, Marcelo rose from his seat in the outdoor plaza and ascended a few steps onto the stage. Hundreds of locals and tourists packed the scenic area next to the beautiful Mission San Luis Obispo de Tolsa, a Spanish mission founded in 1772 by Father Junípero Serra. The warm night, great crowd, and communal enthusiasm for lively music promised an exciting event to come.

Marcelo stood next to the emcee, then shifted uneasily beneath the gazes of so many spectators. He had been called to stages many times in other cities for similar presentations. However, he had never grown accustomed to being the center of attention.

"As our sponsor for this year, Marcelo's selfless and generous contributions to the city demonstrate his virtuous character and love for the arts," the emcee began. "Not only did Marcelo support tonight's jazz festival, he had also donated to the Mission restoration project, the Museum of Art, and the opening of the new wing for the children's museum. Mr. Flores, with tremendous gratitude and admiration from the city of San Luis Obispo, it is my pleasure to present to you this engraved plaque."

The crowd roared its approval through cheers and applause. Marcelo accepted the stunning black marble tablet with words of appreciation and the mayor's signature inscribed on an embedded silver placard. He shifted his feet again when the smiling emcee brought the microphone to his face.

"I can't thank everyone enough," Marcelo said, his voice loud and echoing over the plaza. "Although I live in Avila Beach a short drive away, I've always admired this great city. It's the least I can do to show how grateful I am for your hospitality…even if I'm an undead blood-drinker." Laughter boomed from the crowd, followed by another round of applause. He shook the emcee's hand, waved to the audience, then departed the stage.

Marcelo spent the rest of the event mingling among jazz fans and listening to some excellent music. Afterwards, he left the festival and headed downtown for blood. As the energetic tunes from Poncho Sanchez and his Latin Jazz Band still played in his head, Marcelo hummed one of the melodies with a bounce in his step.

The nighttime streets buzzed in excitement. Concertgoers, shoppers, bar hoppers, and tourists packed the sidewalks and establishments. Eighties music—in his opinion the best after living nearly five hundred years— poured out of a rowdy club as he passed. "The Stroke" by Billy Squier blared on the powerful sound system, and the song promptly replaced the jazz tune dancing in Marcelo's mind.

Crossing the street and turning left, he strolled down a boulevard crammed by a different type of entertainment business. Needles buzzed in tattoo parlors, hookahs churned in smoke shops, mist floated in vape bars, and blood flowed in the blood studio—Marcelo's destination. He stepped into a place called Positive or Negative and headed for the counter.

R&B music spilled from the ceiling speakers. Dull lighting threw shadows over the patrons seated on plush chairs and couches. Several drinks, purses, and smartphones littered the tables. Animated conversation and laughter produced a comfortable atmosphere.

"Hey, Marcelo!" Marie called from behind the desk. With her hair collected in a solid bun and glasses perched on her nose, she looked as beautiful as ever. "Good to see you again."

"Hi, Marie," Marcelo replied. He leaned an elbow on the counter and set the plaque on the wooden top. "Couldn't make it to the jazz festival?"

"No," she answered in an unhappy tone. "I'm sorry I missed your award presentation. I thought the boss would let us close for a couple hours, but here I am. Business is booming, though, and the tips are good tonight."

"I'm glad something worked out for you." He smiled. "Am I late for my appointment?"

"Nope. Your client is actually a bit early." She typed something on the computer. "Her name is Cheryl, blood type A-positive, and your nurse is Abbey. Table twelve. Your award is beautiful, by the way. Very well deserved, Marcelo."

"Thanks! Can I take you dancing tomorrow?"

Marie grinned, then shook her head. "You know I don't date vampires. You're way too old for me."

Marcelo laughed. "Hey, I turned fang-face when I was only eighteen. Although…back in the year fifteen thirty-two."

"Oh, then you're too young for me," Marie said, offering a sly wink. "I'm twenty-three."

"My loss," he replied. "Table twelve?" She nodded, and Marcelo turned away from the counter.

The blood studio called Positive or Negative represented the modern trend of acceptance in the paranormal. Vampires like Marcelo moved freely in society; normal people and the undead lived and worked in mutual respect without fear of harming one another. Countless other supernatural beings also walked among humans. In rare incidents of isolated violence and misunderstanding, exceptions to the norm always existed, yet ordinary communities had long ago adapted to a mystical world that used to endure only in shadow.

Similar to getting tattoos, piercings, or puffing away at a vapor bar with friends, legal and licensed places like Positive or Negative represented cool hangouts for any generation, although the younger crowd seemed to frequent the place. Grab a drink, listen to good music, dance, eat munchies, catch up on gossip, and get a memorable thrill by allowing a vampire to feed on you.

Marcelo moved through the club and nodded to another undead, Keliani, a dark-skinned beauty from the Dominican Republic. A regular at this blood studio, she sat comfortably on a curved sofa with two human males pressed close to her slender form.

Marcelo approached table twelve and found Cheryl, a young girl with green highlights in her jet-black hair. She chatted away on her phone and ignored him as he slipped onto the couch next to her.

Abbey, the uniformed RN, approached and used a tablet to verify Marcelo's credentials and registration in the system. Working off a small rolling tray table, Abbey began preparing Cheryl's arm for insertion of the needle and long tube. The girl continued her tirade into the phone as if nothing else existed around her.

"I know, nitwit," Cheryl said. "I told you I'd be at the blood studio tonight. You never listen—oh yeah, the jazz festival was awesome! You missed out on some good music and food."

The RN nodded when the preparations finished. The sterilization and equipment setup resembled a regular blood bank donation, except the half-pint of A-positive would be consumed by an undead.

Marcelo grasped the thin plastic tube connected to Cheryl's arm and set it between his lips, yet the girl remained buried in her conversation.

"Do you really want to talk about that now?" she asked in disbelief, her voice rising to a high pitch. "I'm in the middle of getting drained, and you're ruining my high!" She then laughed. "Send you a selfie? Really? Fine. If it will keep you from calling me for the next ten minutes, I will."

Cheryl prepped the camera on her smartphone. "Sorry," she said to Marcelo. "My friend is being a real pill tonight. You can begin when you're ready."

"No worries," Marcelo replied. "As an immortal teenager, I remember what it was like to be young."

Cheryl laughed again. "Vampire humor. I love it."

Marcelo carefully drank from the tube, a safe and hygienic method of blood consumption as opposed to a messy, boorish, and uncivilized *bite*. Converting a club donor—or a victim in the street—into a vampire proved impossible unless the drinker allowed the other person to consume some of his or her undead blood in return. Marcelo had never performed such a disgraceful act, not even to those he had loved over the centuries in order to forever remain with them as immortals. His nature did not allow the passing of such a curse, where being categorized as a "beast" and ingesting human blood meant the only way to survive.

Grinning, Cheryl extended her arm to snap the pic. After sending the file to her friend, she leaned back on the couch and closed her eyes.

Eminem and Rihanna's "Monster" played in the background as the blood satiated Marcelo. Or rather, it appeased the demonic entity within him. His human soul had been obliterated long ago, replaced by the ghost of a vanquished demon who craved blood. Marcelo's mind, memories, and experiences remained his; however, his undead body required sustenance in the form of blood, the one aspect the demon spirit would always control.

Every fresh, invigorating drop from Cheryl ran hot inside him, fuel for a complex, preternatural body having incredible senses, speed, and strength. A dozen scents hovered in the air. Without looking, he knew which table had ordered the onion rings, which male wore Polo Red by Ralph Lauren, and which female had a mojito in her hand. Amid the surrounding din of conversation and laughter, the patrons' words and emotions communicated to Marcelo as if he spoke to each person in a private setting. The music pumped and vibrated through him, each note a living reminder of when his heart used to beat.

Beside him, Cheryl's soft breathing floated to his ears. He listened to her heart, its elevated tempo beating its own sweet tune. Euphoria by Calvin Klein caressed her skin, the delightful odor much more pleasant than the sweaty man three couches over. Her rouged lips parted slightly, her breath minty. The green highlights in her black hair reminded him of mint chocolate, the kind given out at restaurants like Olive Garden after a meal.

Her blood flowed between his elongated canine teeth and slipped around his tongue. The taste and sensation felt exhilarating. Cheryl's life, and a piece of her soul, bled into him. A soft moan of pleasure sounded in her throat. He consumed her essence, and it saturated his core to bring life for him in return. Experiencing the girl in a way no one else could, Marcelo would always know Cheryl more intimately than the man she would marry.

"Time up," Abbey announced.

Marcelo released the tube, and Cheryl's eyes fluttered open. "Whoa, dude," she expressed. "That was awesome!"

"I have also enjoyed the opportunity," Marcelo remarked. "Thank you for allowing me to know you, Cheryl."

She nodded. "Thank you for not chewing on my neck."

Marcelo laughed. "Human humor. I also love it. Enjoy the rest of your evening."

The RN finished cleaning Cheryl's arm and packed up the gear. She set a plate of sugar cookies and orange juice on the table, a routine part of the exchange for customers.

Marcelo rose from the couch. About to walk away, a timid hand grasped his wrist. He turned and expected to find Cheryl, but the girl had already returned to her own world with the phone back in her ear. He instead found Abbey, the experienced RN flashing a smile.

"I finish here at two in the morning," she said. "Come pick me up?"

If Marcelo had a functioning heart, it would have skipped as blood rushed to his cheeks in a heated blush. As it stood, he possessed the advantage when confronted by attractive women; his pale, lifeless features allowed him to play it cool.

He took Abbey's hand and kissed the back of it. "I would love to." He paused for a moment. "Bring your uniform?"

The RN's smile widened. "A little cliché, but it's my job. I'll see you in a few hours, handsome."

Marcelo winked, then headed for the counter to say goodbye to Marie and collect his plaque. He wished she had been the one asking to be picked up, but it seemed his dancing days with the pretty girl from Positive or Negative were not meant to be.

Leaving the establishment, he strolled to the parking garage to retrieve his car. He thought a cruise through town would be fun before returning for Abbey. After some hesitation while trying to remember where he left his blue Aston Martin Rapide, he found the vehicle and sat inside.

Marcelo froze. A necklace dangled from his rearview mirror, an odd piece of jewelry he hadn't placed there. A yellow sticky showing the words *Salem, Massachusetts* also hung from the mirror. He took down the necklace and inspected the silver pentagram, a powerful symbol associated with witchcraft.

Marcelo got out of the car and glanced around the parking garage. He didn't see or smell anyone, not even another car driving about. Confused and on guard, he returned to the vehicle and sat behind the wheel.

Who left the necklace here, and why? His car had been locked, which meant the culprit used some special skill to get inside. The person had also left him a message, but Marcelo had no idea what it signified. He didn't appreciate games like this, hated them in fact. The pentagram and note made him feel vulnerable, as if someone had been watching him. Clearly a lot of thought went into this gesture. Unfortunately, the only way to end the game was to play…and win.

Regrettably having to disregard Abbey, Marcelo made the fifteen-minute drive home to Avila Beach. With a population of just under two thousand, the beautiful, secluded, and quiet area fit his preference for peace and privacy. He pulled through the iron gateway of his three-million-dollar home located only a short walk to the sand. The real-estate price tag had been pocket change. After a few hundred years of investments in land, oil, and rail, he had compiled a colossal amount of money following America's birth.

Leaving the Aston Martin in the long, curving driveway, he stepped inside the spacious foyer. A motion sensor activated the crystal chandelier to light the way, and he crossed the white marble tile swirled with blue. Marcelo stepped through the double doors into the carpeted study, then logged onto the computer to make arrangements for a flight tomorrow to Boston.

Afterwards, he packed a suitcase and thought about his trip. As with all vampires, the sun always presented a problem during travel. He would have to take the red-eye out of San Luis, then lay low in Boston until dusk. Afterwards, a rental car would put him in Salem where a hotel waited. From there, Marcelo could only guess what would happen next.

He had never been to Salem, but he knew enough of the town's history from TV shows and books. The tragic witch trials came to mind, and the mysterious pentagram only reinforced the thought. He had actually been present in the New World during the Colonial era, though at the time of the witch trials, he had been roaming the wilderness west of what would eventually be called the Mississippi River.

Marcelo went to the bathroom to wash his hands and face, then paused to look in the mirror. His black hair possessed a "simple casual" style, as the woman at the salon had emphasized. After studying the contours of his face and head, she insisted that this classic look was best for him. She then explained the importance of keeping the hair shorter on the sides and longer at the top. A little gel and a quick brush would do the rest. With great patience, Marcelo had listened and nodded. As an undead, his hair had stopped growing centuries ago, but at least the woman maintained his look for modern times.

In the mirror, green eyes peered back at him, the gaze of a young teenager from Spain who had just become a man and joined the Conquistadors under Francisco Pizarro. His ageless stare had seen nations fall, change hands, and rise again across the world. He had witnessed his own death and rose again with a demonic creature's soul attached to his body like a parasite. Similar to those empires rising and falling, his emotions and attitudes had soared and crumbled over the centuries. Lost lives, vanished loves, mind-blowing changes in society, and incredible advances in technology all flew past him. Marcelo had seen much and learned even more.

Just past midnight, he went outside and walked down San Rafael Street toward the beach. He needed some time to clear his head and ponder the situation regarding the enigmatic necklace showing up in his life. Was he supposed to find a person, or a thing? Did someone wish to hurt him, or worse? Having set foot in numerous countries, a dozen languages rolled off his tongue in ease. And after meeting thousands of people during half a millennium, Marcelo certainly had his fair share of enemies, human or otherwise.

Reaching the deserted beach, he removed the necklace from a pocket and held it up as a cold wave from the Pacific washed around his bare feet. Starlight glinted off the silver encircled star. The pentacle felt old and quite potent, a hidden power dormant within. Marcelo suddenly wanted to cast the thing into the sea.

"What are you dragging me into?" he asked softly. He stared out into the black ocean as another frigid wave crashed onto the wet sand.

Chapter Four

A Modern Witch Hunt

Marcelo had checked into the Hawthorne Hotel, a landmark since 1925 located in the heart of Salem's historic district. The prominent hotel had amassed a fascinating legacy by accommodating many U.S. presidents and Hollywood greats. Having boutique-style quarters, his suite with its eighteenth-century décor possessed unique and graceful character.

Descending from his room, he crossed the elegant, carpeted lobby displaying polished bookcases, fresh potted plants, and gilded mirrors. He walked outside into the cool June night and began the short walk down Hawthorne Boulevard to the Salem Witch Museum on the corner of Washington Square North. Although cruising around in his rented BMW 640i Gran Coupe sounded nice, Marcelo felt glad to stroll through this gorgeous town for a much better experience on foot.

Besides being famous for the Salem Witch Trials, he had read in a brochure that this town had a great history as a popular seaport. In the eighteenth and nineteenth centuries, busy vessels sailed back and forth from Salem to China, the West Indies, Russia, Africa, and other exotic locations. Goods such as codfish, sugar, molasses, tea, and silks represented part of the trade boom. Adding to the town's historical fame, Nathaniel Hawthorne, the author who penned the classic novel *The Scarlet Letter* and had the hotel named after him, had even worked here as a port manager.

Marcelo walked past Salem Common, a large, open area where centuries ago militias trained, and livestock grazed. People strolled in the grass, relaxed on benches, or hung around the stone gazebo near the center of the park. Continuing on, he passed the Stepping Stone Inn and finally reached the imposing Salem Witch Museum with its brown brick, frontal towers, and the overall appearance of a medieval castle.

He reached into a pocket and felt the cool metal of the chain and pentacle. Since finding the clues left in his car, Marcelo had followed his instincts, and in reality, a bit of guesswork. The witch museum seemed like the most logical place to begin.

Present for the late evening tour, several people milled around outside the entrance. Marcelo headed inside and purchased a ticket for the guided exhibition. A bit early, he roamed the gift shop and observed the display of costumes, apparel, trinkets, spell books, and other witch-themed items. He even saw charms and pentacles, though nothing comparable to the old, authentic silver piece in his pocket.

An elderly woman in spectacles announced the commencement of the tour. Marcelo left the gift shop and joined an excited group of tourists. The guide launched into a welcome speech, then led the visitors into an adjacent chamber, the first of thirteen life-sized sets characterizing the dark period of the trials.

The statues dressed in the clothing of the period, the representative decoration, and the guide's dramatic narration brought this tragic occurrence to life. Based on many factual trial documents, the museum displayed dire court scenes and graphic sights of people being hanged from trees.

Throughout this chaotic time in the seventeenth century, Marcelo had stayed away from colonized New England and chose to roam the unexplored wilderness. He had befriended several native tribes, while other clans wanted him burned to ashes. Either way, as a vampire in an unstable and developing world, he felt safer in the remote territories as opposed to hiding among fanatical colonists who hunted witches. He imagined a similar fate for him if those people had discovered an undead in their midst.

The longer the tour lasted, the further Marcelo's mind started to drift. He hadn't seen or heard anything that brought him closer to finding out what the shadowy messenger wanted from him.

As the group moved on to the next scene, a faint vibration buzzed in Marcelo's chest. The sensation felt similar to standing near a large speaker while it blasted club music. However, normal humans would be unable to detect this type of supernatural hum. He understood the vibration's source originated somewhere past a door marked Employees Only.

Marcelo lingered near the back of the group, then slipped away to pass through the marked entry. He moved down a long hallway and paused outside another door. The air hummed as if great machinery worked inside the room, yet he knew no apparatus emitted that drone.

Human smells accompanied the buzz in the air: body sweat, dirty hair, musty clothes, and warm blood. Marcelo realized the vibration prickling his skin came from an individual's aura. A strange person lurked within the room and was quite old…and *powerful.*

Cautious, he opened the door and stepped into a dusty storeroom. He flicked on the light and observed a cluttered array of mannequins, fake trees, crates, coffins, and dozens of other props for the museum displays. In the corner, he approached a timeworn wooden casket and brushed off a large pile of pilgrim costumes and Styrofoam gravestones. He laid a hand on the lid and felt the aura's pulse radiate up his arm.

Grasping a lock hanging from the latch, he twisted it and broke off the metal clasp. He threw back the lid and revealed an ancient, wrinkled woman slumbering inside. Her patchy white hair draped in thin strands. Her liver-spotted skin hung loose. Bony hands and fingers lay over her midsection. A seventeenth century white sleeved, rose-colored waistcoat and wool skirt adorned her body, but this was no costume.

Marcelo gaped in astonishment. Who was this woman? What happened to her? Respiration barely lifted her chest, and he heard her heartbeat. Although she had lain here for a very long time and seemed unable to wake, life flowed strong within her. With the dusty casket stuffed in a corner and buried beneath a pile of junk, he doubted anyone on the museum staff even knew she slept here.

A leather book rested between her high-cut, low-heeled boots. Marcelo picked up the tome and browsed the old pages filled with mystical symbols, potion recipes, ingredients, and the potent words of spell-work.

Apparently, the old woman was a witch in a witch museum. How convenient.

Marcelo removed the pentacle from his pocket. He inspected the object and compared it to a pentagram drawn on one of the pages.

The witch sat up and grabbed his wrist. Milky irises stared in confusion. Hatred then burned through her harsh gaze. Marcelo tried to pull away, but her grip tightened in a crushing force. The hag's mouth opened, and a foul odor wafted as a parched throat uttered hoarse words.

"Give forth my necklace and tome!"

Marcelo finally freed his arm and stepped back. "I will," he said. "No need to get angry." He tossed her the spell book and the pentacle.

The old woman donned the necklace and flipped through the pages of the tome. She then froze. After a moment, she dropped the book on her lap and stared at her withered hands as if she had never seen them before. Mouth agape, she touched her wrinkled face and her shocked expression turned to grief.

"Of a truth, he said I would sleep for over three hundred years," the woman whispered. Trembling, silent tears coursed down her rumpled face. She inspected her worn body and shook her head in denial.

Her hand suddenly flew out. A shaft of light grew between her palm and Marcelo's chest. If he had been alive, his life force would be draining into the woman to charge her with vitality. Lucky for him, he had died centuries ago.

Marcelo smiled. "Sorry, lady. I'm fresh out of juice."

The woman hissed, gray lips parting to reveal yellowed teeth. "Useless undead!" Grief vanished as anger tightened her features. Her cloudy eyes glanced around, then flicked back to Marcelo. "Where am I? Where is Minister Kendrick?"

"You're in Salem," he answered. "I don't know who that person is, but my name is Marcelo Abana Flores. Your necklace brought me to you, though I'm not sure why. Perhaps we can help each other. What's your name?"

The woman climbed out of the casket and nearly lost her balance. Marcelo tried to steady her, but she slapped his hand away. "I care not who you are," she said in scorn. "Hitherto, my only concern is killing Minister Kendrick."

"If you tell me who he is, I might—"

"I do not have time for incompetent vampires!" she shouted.

She clapped her hands once, and a jet of fire sprayed toward Marcelo. The flames scorched the side of his face and right shoulder. Stumbling backwards, he tripped over a carton and fell onto the cement floor. He caught a glimpse of the witch as she raced out the door.

Standing, Marcelo grabbed a pile of sheets and snuffed out the flames that had caught on some of the stage props. He grimaced as the charred, damaged skin on his face, neck, and shoulder slowly restored. The undead flesh molded to its original state; blisters faded and inflamed areas grew smooth. A sustained and more intense blast from the woman's fire may have destroyed him, one of the very few things that could. He would have to be careful as he chased her down.

Hurrying away from the storeroom, a hundred thoughts bounced in his head. He had followed the clues and awakened the witch, but what came next? Someone had the answers. Could it be this Minister Kendrick?

Whatever the story, Marcelo vowed to solve the mystery of his connection to the woman. To accomplish that he would have to help her and hope she wouldn't incinerate him through anger and confusion. The old woman had been dragged into this situation as well. Based on her Colonial dress and demeanor, this modern world would be huge and terrifying for someone who had allegedly been locked away for hundreds of years.

Chapter Five

Insatiable Vengeance

Lost in a living nightmare, Sybil's mind spiraled out of control as she escaped the room where she woke and ran down a hallway. Minister Kendrick's words had come true. She had slept for hundreds of years, and her body had aged into that of an old woman. She regained consciousness in bizarre surroundings and a vampire her only company.

Sybil battled panic as her boots echoed on the hard floor. Instead of lanterns, candles, or torches, some sort of odd, stationary lights burned overhead. Reaching a door, she burst through it and screamed at the sight of women hanging from a tree. A ghastly cemetery lay nearby. Not far from there, angry people crammed a courtroom where a terrified girl stood on trial.

Sobbing, Sybil realized she had not escaped the terrible witch hunts after all. Even centuries later, girls were still being tried and executed. Fear welled and she looked around for an escape, but something seemed very wrong. None of the people in court talked or moved. The men working the ladders and nooses also stood frozen in place. Slowly, she walked toward the tree and noticed the false faces of the deceased, like masks. The women's bodies were also not real, only stuffed clothing.

What in the world was happening? Where was she?

"Oh, cool!" a voice called. "A witch came out."

A strange light flashed. Sybil turned and saw a group of bizarrely dressed people staring at her. Many of them held up odd rectangular devices. Another light flashed from one of the things as the crowd pointed them at her.

"She must be a new part of the show," a man said. "I don't remember this from last year."

Wearing a look of confusion, a woman dressed in a uniform approached Sybil. "Are you a new hire? Your costume is great, but this isn't part of the script and you're interfering with my tour group."

The door Sybil had run through flew open and the vampire glanced around. She left the crowd and snuck toward a lobby full of people. Across the way, a large door stood open and revealed the outside draped in night. She dashed past the exit and shock nearly made her collapse.

The environment bustled, a hundred things she had never seen or heard before. Roaring like lions and built of iron, a dozen horseless carriages raced by on a hard black street. Lacking fire, false lights blazed high overhead on tall poles. Eerie, pounding music shrieked from the iron carriages as they passed. A terrifying bird raced across the darkened sky, glowing, screaming in a thunderous rumble.

And the people—they would not stop staring and flashing those little lights at her.

"Hey," a man called. "I love the hag outfit. Can my kids get a picture with you before the next tour?"

"Leave me be!" Sybil screamed.

She ran toward a shadowed knot of trees across the street. The iron carriages squealed and growled as she passed. Glancing over a shoulder, the irritating vampire emerged from the building and spotted her. What did he want? Kendrick must have sent him. Why else would the undead creature have her pentacle? The vampire had acted innocent, but she didn't believe him, not after what she had gone through. Right now, Sybil's stunned mind only wanted to escape. Fighting tears and madness, she desired peace and privacy before losing her wits.

The tiniest sliver of the Old Crone's waning moon hung overhead. In two days, a dark new moon would preside in the heavens followed by the waxing moon of the Maiden. Tonight's convenient waning moon represented a time for spells to banish, reverse, or diminish—a glimmer of hope as Sybil uttered a spell.

"Old Crone, forever known, let not the vampire see what ought not be shown!"

Sybil passed under the darkened tree line. Hugging the tome to her chest, she leaned against a trunk and tried to catch her breath. The vampire caught up and slowed to a walk beneath the canopy, glancing around. His gaze settled right on her…then passed as he moved on. Her temporary cloaking spell had worked.

The slender, black-haired undead possessed the appearance of a teenager. Instead of the hard, calculated look of a predator on the hunt, worry softened his face. Perhaps knowing she couldn't have gotten far, he patrolled the area beneath the trees, sniffing the air and pausing in confusion.

After several moments he finally left the area. Sybil sank to the ground and curled into a fetal position. Her old body reacted cruelly as the adrenaline began to fade. Agony flared in her joints. Her brittle bones ached, and sore muscles throbbed.

But worst of all, her heart bled under intense emotional pain.

According to Kendrick, centuries had passed while Sybil slept. But to her, losing Constance had only happened moments ago. She still felt her beloved friend's soft curls in her fingers and saw Constance's hazel eyes shining over the rim of a teacup.

Sybil cried into the dirt. The passing carriages on the nearby street drowned out her tormented wails. Minister Kendrick's wrinkled face and yellow eyes swam before her. The ignorant mob danced and cheered as Constance swung from the tree. Sybil's hand clawed the ground in frustration. Anger and grief agitated her insides until she felt sick.

Trembling, she sat up and wiped her eyes and mouth. "I shall destroy them all," she whispered.

Sybil hadn't forgotten the final spell she cast, the one that had branded the hands of those responsible for her friend's death. Fueled by Sybil's centuries-old wrath, the powerful ash-stain magic would have passed on to the marked ones' offspring. She would hunt the mob's descendants in this strange world and eliminate them— the only way to satisfy her rampant need for vengeance. The horde's hateful spirit ran in their children's veins, and even after several generations, the blood price for Constance's sacrifice must be paid.

Injustice had been a large part of Sybil's life. Throughout her childhood, she had lived in fear while hiding and moving from place to place to avoid witch-hunters. Her mother had been slain during the attempt to escape England. Bridget Bishop, Constance, and certainly other girls had been killed in Salem Village. The cycle of violence and terror haunted her while traversing oceans and even across time itself, over three centuries to be exact. The persistent fear, relentless suffering, and having everything she loved torn away had poisoned Sybil until one clear path remained. A system of justice had to be created, a hate-filled movement with blood certain to stain her hands.

Standing, she hissed as pain lashed throughout her aching body. She strolled around the grove, wincing, then stretched to work some of the kinks and soreness out of her limbs. Afterwards, she moved back to the edge of the tree line and looked out at the busy street. People sat inside the carriages as they passed. She wondered how the things moved without being pulled by an animal. She studied the tall lamps and their false fire. Another noisy bird—though not a bird—soared high in the sky with blinking lights.

Sybil had no idea what year she had awoken in. A few hundred had passed, perhaps making this the twenty-first century. Novel inventions, advancements in society, and modern culture were only some of the wonders—and terrors—to expect in her new world.

Her mind spun, and she placed a hand over her chest. She took a deep, calming breath. The insane situation threatened to crush her beneath bewilderment, denial, and fear. She had lost her entire life in an instant. Now old and withered, how much time did she have left?

Searching for internal strength, she reached into her waistcoat and pulled out the pentacle. The necklace represented all she had left of her mother. Certainly, no proper burial had occurred, a place where Sybil could visit and connect to her mother. She kissed the symbol and thought of how courageous and resilient Olivia had been.

"Please watch over me, Mother," Sybil said softly. "Time and space stand between us, but you are forever in my heart." She tucked the pentacle safely back inside.

Peering across the street to study the building she had run out of, Sybil gasped. The sign on the front read: Salem Witch Museum. She then laughed until tears leaked from her eyes. In seventeenth century England, the word "museum" was used to describe a collection of curiosities, such as John Tradescant's natural history objects at the University of Oxford. It seemed witches had become a thing of curiosity, something to have on display. The fake people and witch trial scenes inside the building made sense now.

The humor subsided as powerful anger replaced her mirth. Witches had been reduced to entertainment. These modern citizens treated real people and tragedies as a simple curiosity. She imagined visitors smiling in the museum as they learned about the past. No one in this era could understand the horror of the real trials, of watching loved ones murdered. The descendants Sybil hunted stood emotionally detached from what their forefathers had done. That separation from reality and the unwarranted innocence fueled her rage even more.

Having a dozen things to plan, an overwhelming hunger suddenly gripped Sybil. Her stomach growled, and she licked her lips. It seemed her body craved nourishment after sleeping for so long. She also realized her colonial outfit did not match the modern style, probably why the museum visitors had stared at her. She needed to blend in, but for now, food dominated her cravings instead of clothes.

Leaving the grove with her tome tucked under an arm, she strolled down random streets and ignored the odd glances from the occasional pedestrian. She followed her nose and eventually came across an eating establishment. Wonderful smells of hot food wafted from inside. Bella Verona Ristorante, the sign outside read.

Her mouth watered and stomach roared again. Thinking of nothing but food, Sybil stepped inside and found the place bursting with patrons. Steaming pastas, meats in red sauce, and buttered bread on dozens of plates overwhelmed her. Not having any coin or things to trade, she moved to a table and set down her book, then picked up someone's plate and shoved food into her mouth.

Etiquette and manners flew out the window as Sybil ate, her body quivering in need for sustenance. Disoriented from waking in this strange place and having no answers to her dilemma, for the moment she only cared about the basics as her body craved simple human need.

She set the empty plate on the table and lifted a glass of water to gulp down. Sighing in contentment, she now registered the gawking faces and the stunned couple sitting at the table.

A female in a uniform approached. "You can't take other people's food," she said. "The manager will fix you a to-go box if you leave now. If not, we'll have to call the police."

"Truly, there is no need to summon the night watch," said Sybil. "I shall leave, I warrant. But first tell me where Minister Kendrick dwells."

"I don't know who that is," the woman replied.

"Please, just leave," a heavyset man said as he drew near and extended a container to Sybil.

She took the box—more delicious smells from inside—and started to ask the patrons about Kendrick when the large man grabbed her by the elbow. After everything she had been through, Sybil reacted out of instinct. She threw out her hand, and black smoke from her palm blasted the man's face.

"Sleep!" she hollered.

The man collapsed. His body crashed onto the table, then rolled onto the floor in a clatter of shattering crockery and startled screams.

Sybil ran out the door with her book and the food box. The last thing she needed was the night watch throwing her in a cell. Heading down another random street, her old body caused her to slow. She rested against the side of a building, panting, and took a moment to collect her thoughts.

The sleep spell marked another example of something Sybil had never been capable of before. The power had welled inside her and burst in an instant. The reaction occurred similar to the sudden, strong magic she had cast in Salem Village after losing Constance. Earlier during her escape from the museum, the fire she had thrown at the vampire had also been new and instinctive.

Could this be the power Kendrick had spoken of right before putting her to sleep? *During your slumber, your abilities will grow even more potent. Like a fine wine, your body and spirit need time in the cellar to turn out their best.* What did the deranged minister want from her? Whatever the reason, Sybil vowed to use her new abilities to crush the life out of Kendrick and the descendants of the witch-hunting mob.

After feeling rested, she continued walking until she reached the water's edge. Several moored vessels bobbed next to a long pier. Nostalgia struck as the smell of salty ocean and the sound of lapping water brought memories of her voyage across the Atlantic from England. Sybil thought of happy periods growing up with her mother and of memorable times alongside Constance in Salem Village before the witch hysteria began.

Perched on a long, thin finger of land, a small modern lighthouse in the distance caught her attention. She strolled toward it in hope of achieving isolation from this peculiar world. She also desired a better view of the night-darkened sea.

The sign identified the place as Derby Wharf Light Station. Sybil stood on the tip of the finger and gazed out over the black water. After setting her things down, she removed her coif and a soft breeze tousled her straight hair, now thin and white as it hung to mid-back. Across the bay, mysterious lights glinted along the shore, more than likely those false lanterns that seemed to shine everywhere, even inside the lighthouse.

"May I join you?" a voice asked out of nowhere.

Sybil whirled, and her heart thundered while anticipating a fight. With the cloaking spell expired, the vampire from the museum had found her.

Chapter Six

Unsteady Alliance

Marcelo threw his hands up as if deflecting a blow. "Whoa! Sorry, I didn't mean to frighten you. Please don't burn my face off."

"How did you find me, and wherefore?" the old witch asked in irritation. "Hitherto, you have been in pursuit since yonder museum."

The woman maintained her aggressive posture. Marcelo hoped she wouldn't attack him as the witch had already proven capable of inflicting harm.

"I followed the police sirens and interviewed witnesses," he said. "An elderly woman running around in pilgrim clothing while turning Salem upside down is not something that happens every day."

Her eyes widened. "Is the night watch coming hither? Are you handing me over to Kendrick?"

Marcelo shook his head. "That's the second time you've mentioned that name. Look, I really want to help you. Back near my home, someone put your necklace in my car with a note that said Salem, but I don't know why. After traveling here in search of answers, I stumbled into that storeroom at the museum and found you asleep in the coffin. I'm just as lost as you are on the matter. So let's help each other, okay?"

The witch remained silent, more than likely fighting an internal battle of trust. Marcelo surmised the woman felt utterly alone, overwhelmed, and desired to find answers just as much as he did. Would that be enough for her to confide in him?

"Your modern prattle is strange, though I conceive its meaning," she said. "If we truly strive for the same purpose, then it would behoove us to toil together. However, I shall destroy you the moment you attempt to harm me."

"I expect nothing less," Marcelo replied.

"Then you are a learned man," the witch said. "You already presented your name, Marcelo. Mine is Sybil Radella Cotterill."

"It's a pleasure to meet you," he said. "I believe Sybil means prophetess. Cotterill must be cottager, but Radella eludes me. What does that signify?"

"Elfin counselor."

Marcelo grinned. "Like in *Lord of the Rings?*"

Sybil furrowed her brow and shook her head. "I do not conceive what that means. Do elfin lords dwell nearby?"

Marcelo laughed. "Never mind, it's just a movie reference I'll teach you about later. But you do have a gorgeous name." He studied her for a moment. "Sybil, upon waking you looked at your hands and whispered something about a few hundred years. Was that how long you were in the casket?"

Tears welled in Sybil's eyes as she picked up a small box that smelled of food. She also collected the spell book Marcelo recognized from before.

"Yes," she said quietly. "To me, I was a girl of eighteen only moments agone. Then Minister Kendrick closed my eyes, and I opened them to discover myself in this condition, in this era."

Marcelo couldn't imagine the disorientation and pain tormenting Sybil. He read something in her sorrowed features, a greater despair that signified the agony of loss. Her hands trembled as she held her things, shoulders slumped in grief. Besides waking up to find herself older, the poor woman must have suffered some horrible trauma. As for him, having died and undergone a terrifying transformation, Marcelo shared a similar experience and bond with Sybil. Not having been able to help himself, he would do anything to support his new acquaintance while they worked together to unravel this mystery.

"Let's go back to my hotel," Marcelo suggested. "On the way, I'll get you some modern clothes and you can clean up in the room. When you are refreshed, and willing, I'd like to hear more of your story. We'll discover the clues together and find a way to make things right."

"Thank you, Marcelo. Of a truth, you seem quite different from the vampires I met in England years agone. I only had a fair sight of a couple, but they were rather on the feral side."

"Times are certainly different now," he said. "I'll have to teach you everything about the twenty-first century." He reached for her box and tome. "May I carry these for you?"

She smiled and handed over the items. "I seem to have met a polite vampire. Forthwith I truly conceive these modern times are different. As for your name,

Marcelo means hammer. Abana is made of stone, and Flores means flowers."

"Hey, not bad!" Marcelo remarked as they walked away from the lighthouse. "I'm from Spain, but my story is for another time. Right now, it's all about the *Sleeping Beauty* witch."

"Sleeping beauty? You also said some strange words earlier—a *moovy,* and a car."

"I'll explain the movie stuff later. As for my car, it's one of those…metal horseless carriages you see rolling around."

"I believe I understand."

The smell of lasagna drifted to Marcelo's nose, and he glanced at the food box. "Bella Verona." He laughed. "I heard you knocked out the manager after he gave you some food to-go. I guess I won't be taking you there tomorrow for dinner."

Sybil laughed, and Marcelo thought it was the greatest sound he had heard all night. It relieved him to see her in a better mood. "My BMW—my car—is parked nearby. After you escaped from the museum, I went back to the hotel and hopped in my ride to search for you. We'll stop by a clothing store. It's late, so hopefully one is still open."

Reaching Derby Street near Jaho Coffee and Tea, Marcelo walked to the 640i Gran Coupe and opened the door for Sybil. He tried not to smile at the terrified look on her face.

"Go ahead and sit," he offered. "It's safe."

After hesitating, Sybil maneuvered inside and sat as rigid as a soldier.

"I'm going to help you with the seatbelt," said Marcelo. "Watch how it's done, then you can do it next time."

"Truly, what makes you believe I shall climb aboard this contraption again?" she asked.

Marcelo buckled her in. "After some cruising with the windows down on this fine evening, you'll be begging me for rides."

He stepped around the vehicle and sat behind the steering wheel, then dug his phone out of a pocket. "This is a smartphone. Think of it as a tome with near limitless information inside. I'm going to find us a clothing store. Check this out."

After a few taps on Google, he discovered The Boutique close by on Front Street. "See? Their website says, 'We provide the perfect balance of casual and chic'. Anyway, I'll buy you a phone tomorrow and show you much more."

Sybil's mouth hung open the entire time he showed her the phone. "That thing is remarkable, I warrant! It is so small and resourceful. And hitherto, I am hefting this cumbersome book around."

"That's technology for you. Small, resourceful, and easy to lose." Marcelo fired the engine and drove away. He looked at Sybil; she had turned white as a sheet. "Sit back and relax. Aren't you used to flying around on brooms?"

"I do not conceive your meaning."

"Never mind. Bad joke."

Sybil remained stiff and silent the entire way to the Boutique. Marcelo had to keep glancing at her to ensure the witch hadn't passed out. He pulled in front of the shop and prepared to step out.

"You should wait in here," he told her. "The cops…the night watch, might still be looking for you. I'll have to guess on your size, but we should be fine."

Marcelo entered the shop and received a warm welcome from the young woman behind the counter. With the store about to close and his haste to get Sybil out of the public eye, he didn't have time to browse. He selected a few dresses, blouses, pants, sleepwear, shoes, purse, and sunhat.

After placing the bags in the back seat of the BMW, he checked on Sybil and found she seemed a bit more relaxed.

"I hope you like what I purchased," he said. "The garments may not fit your taste, but at least no one will mistake you for an extra from *The Scarlet Letter* movie."

Sybil clucked her tongue. "Your modern speech remaineth quite odd. Another *moovy* reference? You always speak in that manner with a silly smirk on your face. Forthwith explain what *moovys* are and what the references signify. Otherwise, your fancy for humor is worthless if I do not conceive it."

"Not understanding them, and the look on your face after I say it, makes it funnier," Marcelo quipped. "But we'll have a movie marathon night for some quality education. It'll be a blast!"

They drove off, and Sybil even leaned back in the seat a little. Reaching the Hawthorne Hotel, Marcelo led the way to his room and escorted Sybil inside. "The decoration is from the eighteenth century," he commented. "The suite is not that big, but it fits the hotel's theme. The main room is there, where you'll be sleeping. I'll draw you a hot bath, and you can relax. Are you still hungry? I can order room service, or you can chow on your Bella's."

"Hunger does not ail me," Sybil replied. "What about your food? Vampires may be more sophisticated forthwith, but do you still…" She pointed to one of her canine teeth.

Marcelo smiled as he placed the take-out box in the mini-fridge next to the dry bar. "Yes, we still do that. I mean no! We don't go around biting people on the street. At least most of us don't. There are other, safer means for us to drink blood. I had my sustenance before arriving in Salem so I'm good for a couple days." He went into the bathroom to fill the tub.

"Where shall you sleep?" she called from the living room sofa. "Or do you?"

"Sometimes I do, but it's actually more of a light doze." Marcelo poured soap granules into the running water to create a frothy bubble bath. "The sofa you're sitting on is where I'll rest."

After the preparations, he called Sybil into the bathroom. "I won't question your bathing habits of the seventeenth century," he began, "but I'll show you how to enjoy a hot soak in the tub by modern standards." He dried his hands and demonstrated the use of the loofah, shampoo, and some lotions. "There are also plenty of towels," he finished. "Take your time while I hang up your new outfits."

As Sybil emerged from the bath wearing her new sleepwear, Marcelo had finished preparing her room. He sat using his phone to read about a local charity called the Bright Star Foundation.

"How are you feeling?" he asked.

"I fare well," she replied, sitting next to him on the sofa. "Truly, the hot water felt wonderful and I almost fell asleep." She observed the phone in his hand. "What are you doing with the modern tome…the smartphone?"

"I'm using it to send money to this charity." He showed her the screen. "It's pretty amazing. Two sisters created the Bright Star Foundation. The oldest was seventeen and the younger fifteen when they first started. They visit nursing homes, places where some ill or disabled elderly live. Some of the residents have no family, so these girls cheer them up using animals, pass the time doing activities, and give the patients presents for holidays. The foundation also provides education to orphans and other children in need."

"Very impressive," said Sybil. "Yonder two girls are incredible, I warrant, and I am certain they create happiness for a lot of people. Thereof what you are doing is just as wonderful, Marcelo. Giving forth money to strangers is very noble, and I admire you for it."

Marcelo shrugged. "Thank you, Sybil. It's just something I do."

"Just something you do? Curiosity overcomes me to know wherefore. In Salem Village, I would do everything possible to bring forth a good crop for the people. I used my magic in secret, lest I be tried and executed as a witch if caught in the fields. But no one ever conceived of what I did or expressed gratitude for it. I often asked myself wherefore I ought to help these strangers who would do harm unto me."

Sybil paused and shook her head, her old face distant in recollection. "Truly, I did it because I desired to live a normal life," she continued. "I dwelled among the townsfolk, traded with them, had conversations, and simply acted as their fellow citizen. But yonder folk were not my friends, nor anyone I could trust. Any one of them would hand me over to the constable if they discovered I was a witch. Of a truth, aiding them with the crop was my pathetic attempt to be normal and contribute to society…all while hiding in the shadows."

She suddenly looked apologetic, then touched Marcelo's arm. "Truly, I do not mean to say that is why you help people you have never met, Marcelo. Please do not misunderstand me. My actions those years agone were just…well, my way of making a contribution, like you."

Marcelo sat stunned. Sybil had nearly spoken his own thoughts aloud. He slipped an arm around her frail shoulders, and she leaned into him.

"You're actually right, Sybil," he began. "My donations are not just absent things I do. Over the centuries, I've also been hunted, hated, and ridiculed for what I am. But today's culture has changed as you've seen for yourself. The supernatural is tolerated and welcome, but I am no human. Despite walking alongside humans in stores, raising glasses with them, conversing, or going to events, I'm still not part of their society. Beneath the smiles and handshakes, it's no secret I've slaughtered countless people for survival over the years. Citizens on the street look at me a little odd, and act differently when I join their group. Whether it's intentional or subconscious, it's human nature."

Marcelo stared at the wall, his mood somber at the confession he was about to make. "I feel…I feel alone, Sybil. Just as you did, I also hide in the shadows, both literally and figuratively. Sunlight makes it a necessity. The invisible wall separating human from monster makes it inevitable."

Sybil ran a comforting hand along his back. A moment ago, he had been the one listening to and reassuring her; now the roles had reversed. He smiled and patted her knee.

"I'm supposed to be the one helping you," he said. "Ever since the paranormal and humanity united, I've never admitted these feelings to anyone. We just met, but I feel relaxed around you. I believe we have much in common, Sybil, and that makes for easy conversation."

Her wrinkled face lifted in a smile. "My heart feels the same way, Marcelo. I woke from yonder coffin surrounded by madness, and thus believed I would be alone and terrified of everything. Being afraid hath not changed, but I was never alone. You have been there since the beginning."

She took his hand and pressed it between her gnarled ones. "Thank you for taking good care of me hitherto. I do not wish to cause you trouble, I warrant. I have dragged you hither from your home, and we still do not have any answers as to what is occurring."

"You're not any trouble, Sybil. Like the Bright Star Foundation, you are my charity now and my only concern is your safety. Someone out there is playing us both, and together we'll overcome this. In the museum, you said you wanted to kill Minister Kendrick. Tell me about him and your story of how you ended up in the casket. I think some more background is a good place to start."

"I shall," said Sybil. She pointed to the dry bar. "But may we consume some of yonder wine while we speak? I am going to need it, I warrant."

Marcelo poured drinks and listened to the witch's story. He sat tense on the edge of his seat, appalled at what Sybil had gone through. Her words transported him to the seventeenth century, and he experienced her adversity and pain. After escaping England, she had lived right here in Salem and survived the witch trials of 1692. The young girl had lost much and suffered more.

Sybil finished speaking. Her look remained distant, faded eyes buried in the past and wrinkled features warped by despair. Marcelo handed her a tissue, and she wiped her eyes.

"My face may not show it, but of a truth, I feel so much better," said Sybil. "I needed to share my experience with someone, to release anger and grief from my heart. You spoke true, we do have a lot in common, and you conceive my pain. You have experienced death, and over the years I am certain you have lost loved ones as well. I appreciate your attention, Marcelo, and your being with me."

Sybil's feelings matched his from before, when he had experienced a connection to her through shared circumstances. Marcelo strengthened his vow to aid her, to eliminate the tears and replace each drop with a smile. For now, he shared her contentment in knowing her heart beat more freely.

He poured each of them another glass of wine, their third. Alcohol didn't affect him, but he enjoyed the tart and sweet taste of this particular red. "This monster of a man, Kendrick. He took the pentacle from you, and it ended up in my car. I then brought the necklace to

Salem, and you awoke. I'm confident Kendrick is lurking around while setting up this entire affair, but to what end?"

Sybil sipped from her glass. "I know not. He compared my magic ability to fine wine in the cellar and said I needed time to develop my power. He wanted me to grow strong, and truly I have. My new skills are unrefined, but I am able to do things I never imagined hitherto."

"Kendrick also wanted a vampire to find you, but why me?" Marcelo wondered. "I live across the country, and there are several blood suckers right here in Salem. Any one of them could have received the pentacle."

"Perhaps Kendrick needed to summon the least intelligent vampire."

Marcelo stared in surprise, and Sybil erupted in laughter. "Forgive me, I believe it is the wine," she said. "I fancied a bit of humor."

Grinning, Marcelo poured out more. "Good one. Let's hope your wit gets better with another round."

Sybil clinked her glass against his. "There is a favor I wish to ask, but you have already done enough for me," she began. "It shall not be easy, and it shall take time away from our investigation."

Marcelo waved a dismissive hand. "Don't worry about any of that. We'll find time to play *Sherlock Holmes* when necessary—yes, another movie reference. Tell me what you need, and I'll make it happen."

Sybil sighed and ran a finger around the rim of her glass. "This may sound silly, but my heart wonders if my family's descendants still dwell in Salem. It would please me to find out, to at least conceive if the family name hath survived."

"You mean from your sister and two brothers in your story, who traveled with you and Constance from England," Marcelo replied. "That's not silly at all. It's a great idea. Locating their descendants will make you feel more at home. If you do have family around, perhaps you can see them and present yourself as a distant relative. Your pentacle and knowledge of the family line will be proof enough."

Sybil's face brightened. "Truly, that would be wonderful. Do you believe it is possible? I can perform blood location magic, but I would need a sundry of supplies for spell casting. Do those materials exist in this era?"

"Of course, and you're in the heart of witch territory. Google will show us the way." Marcelo took out his phone, but Sybil snatched it from his hand.

"Allow me!" she exclaimed. "I wish to see if this tome of technology shall work for me."

Behind her aged look, Marcelo admired the spirited youth of a teenage girl. Eagerness and delight danced in her cloudy eyes. She ran her fingers over the phone, turned it over, and marveled at the device's features everyone else took for granted. Her wide smile reflected the adventurous adolescent inside, trapped by a worn and broken old body.

"This is your first test of the modern century," said Marcelo. "Use your finger to type out 'witchcraft stores in Salem'…no, right here…yep! Just like that. Now press this search button, and let's see what pops up."

After a moment, Marcelo read from the page. "Look, there's the Crow Haven Corner, apparently the oldest witch shop in Salem. Occult books, herbs, crystals, spell kits, candles, and much more. Should suffice for what you need, I would think."

"Yes, that sundry shall do," said Sybil. "Let us go forthwith."

"They're closed. We'll just have to wait until tomorrow. But the worst part is how near the store is to the hotel. It's right across the street, which means no car ride for you. Takes the fun out of the experience."

"I am not displeased by that," Sybil replied. "The less time in your carriage, the better. But speaking of witchcraft supplies, my heart wonders about the witches of this modern world. Judging from the fair sight I had of yonder museum, and conceiving that magic shops are a normal matter, what kind of witches are in practice today? Where do they dwell? Are they truly accepted by society?"

Marcelo finished his wine. He gestured with the glass, and after Sybil nodded, he refilled both their drinks. "Witches are certainly accepted by society, although there will always be people who ridicule a lifestyle they know nothing about. But the persecutions and hunts ended long ago. And witches can be anyone. The nurse at the clinic, the worker at the store, the server at the coffee shop.

"As for what type, there are dozens," Marcelo continued. "Solitary, secular, hereditary, traditional, Hellenic, green, dream, kitchen—"

"Stop forthwith! You are making my head ache. Wherefore so many?"

"It's difficult to say, but there are hundreds of books and websites—from the tome of technology—that claim to know the original style of witchcraft from ancient history. There are even arguments over whether witchcraft is a religion or a practice. From what I've seen over the centuries, and correct me if I'm wrong, there is no singular, real way to perform witchcraft. A person simply does it in whatever form suits them. 'Each to his or her own', is what the cliché term says, meaning everyone does what suits them. In this modern world of endless critics, I believe that term fits best for every aspiring or experienced witch out there."

"Well, you are not incorrect, I warrant," said Sybil. "It pleased Constance and I to have our own style, and we learned from each other over the years agone. In England, if you inquired ten witches for advice on how to bless a crop, you would receive ten different answers. Thus, I shall believe your…cliché statement holds truth."

Sybil yawned into a fist. "The wine is closing my eyes forthwith. After slumbering in a box for centuries, going to sleep is not something I desire. But perhaps a little rest shall not harm me before our important task on the morrow."

"I'm excited to help you find your family's descendants," said Marcelo. "I don't know if any of them will be in Salem or even Massachusetts, but I'll take you anywhere you need to go."

"I ought not allow hope to overwhelm me. Perhaps I shall not find any of them at all."

Marcelo put the glasses and near-empty bottle away. "We'll try, and that's the important thing. Get some rest, Sybil. Tomorrow you'll have an amazing breakfast and then we'll be on our way."

She stood and planted a kiss on his cheek. "Shall you rest as well, your doze?"

"Just for a short while. I might see if there are any movies on first."

The fatigue vanished from Sybil's face. Her eyes widened, and she glanced around. "Truly, you have those? You never said anything. Show me a *moovy* forthwith!"

Marcelo laughed and gestured to the sofa. "Have a seat." He turned on the flat screen, searched through the menu, and found an old western with Clint Eastwood.

Sybil sat frozen as the movie played. Complete astonishment dominated her features. Sometimes she laughed, or shrieked in surprise, and asked question after question. Halfway through the film, Marcelo noticed her eyelids growing heavy. She spoke less, and her body had melted into the cushions. Soon her breathing changed to the slow, steady rhythm of sleep.

Marcelo turned off the TV and carried Sybil to her room. He tucked her into bed and closed the door softly behind him.

Chapter Seven

The Retribution Begins

Nightmares about Constance's death plagued Sybil's sleep. She woke under a blanket of misery, which set her tone for the day. Last night the bed had felt luxurious, but rest eluded her. At least the wonderful breakfast of eggs, hashed browns, and pancakes settled comfortably in her belly. Dressed in her new clothes, she crossed the hotel lobby with Marcelo at her side.

"Are you certain your clothing shall protect you from yonder sun?" Sybil asked.

Marcelo adjusted his long sleeves and gloves. A wide-brimmed hat, sunglasses, and a scarf added to his attire. "I've gone out like this before. I naturally try to avoid daytime movement, but today it's a necessity."

Sybil smiled to herself. He looked ridiculous, but evading direct sunlight was essential for the undead. She appreciated his help and valued his willingness to brave the danger just to accompany her to the store.

However, guilt crept into her heart as she thought about last night. While telling her story, she had been truthful about every detail except for the addition of two brothers and a sister accompanying her to Salem. The request to locate her family descendants posed as a cover for finding Constance's murderers. Being dishonest turned Sybil's stomach, yet she had to use Marcelo, her only link to this world and a means to fulfill her desire for revenge. He would refuse to help her if he knew the truth.

Leaving the lobby and moving south from the Hawthorne, they crossed Essex Street and entered the store called Crow Haven Corner. Overwhelmed by the extensive display of items, Sybil couldn't believe how easy it was to find everything she needed. Back in the seventeenth century, growing and gathering herbs, hunting for stones and minerals, molding candles, and even locating ink and quill had provided challenges to performing witchcraft. Days and weeks would be spent preparing for the simplest of spells. Now, she could purchase the necessities in only a few moments.

Browsing the store, she looked with interest at the other customers. Young girls and boys accompanied by friends, or older men and women moved casually about. Other clients didn't seem to be witches at all. Those individuals only seemed curious as they played with the items or asked the attendant trivial questions.

"I don't see many vampires in here," said a smiling, middle-aged woman clutching a paper sack of candles. "Or out in the daytime, for that matter. You must be working on something important."

"I'm helping my friend with a location spell," Marcelo commented. "We hope to find some members of her family."

"You do not need to prattle to strangers about our business," Sybil cut in.

"Hey, I'm just making conversation," Marcelo replied. "No need to get upset."

The woman's cheeks bloomed red. "No, she's right. I come here often and love meeting new people, but sometimes I'm too nosy. Please forgive me. Maybe I can assist you with something?"

"I do not require help from useless amateurs," Sybil responded. "Go away."

The woman's mouth fell open. Marcelo stared in shock.

An unexpected rage had flared in Sybil's gut. The other woman didn't deserve this rudeness, but Sybil couldn't help it. These modern witches seemed so pampered and at ease with everything. In the same way Sybil had felt anger toward the witch museum, these witches today could never comprehend what she had gone through—the torment and nightmare of the hunts. No present-day witch had seen their beloved friend choke to death in a noose or had watched their mother die at the hands of crooked men.

The non-witch shoppers also irritated Sybil. An abrupt hatred had obliterated her initial interest. The laughing, curious outsiders carelessly handled and played with ancient symbols and powerful tools that some witches in Sybil's time had spent fortunes on or died trying to acquire. Now the items sat on shelves to be mocked and disrespected by modern fools. Even the real witches in the store appeared ignorant, like this intruding woman. How could these spoiled and naïve people compare themselves to Sybil, an old-world spellcrafter whose abilities had nearly risen to those of a deity?

"I…I truly apologize," the woman stammered. "It must be obvious, I really am a bit of an amateur." She produced a small card from a pocket and held it out to Sybil. "I'm starting a new coven. Maybe you can stop by sometime. I make tasty pies and love to cook on the grill. I'd love to learn from you. My name is Grace, by the way."

When Sybil failed to grasp the card, Marcelo did instead. "Thank you, Grace. My name is Marcelo. I hope you enjoy the rest of your day."

After Grace left the store, the atmosphere of the shop grew hot and stuffy. The packed shelves, limited space, and the other customers milling about crowded Sybil until she found it difficult to breathe. She handed Marcelo her basket filled with ingredients. "Please make the purchase. I shall wait outside."

On the sidewalk, Sybil inhaled the fresh air, though it did nothing to calm her. She sat on the curb and pulled her knees into her chest, then lowered her head and cried.

A short time later, Marcelo's gloved hand rested on her shoulder. "Let's go back to the room, Sybil. You've had a rough day, and it's not even lunchtime. Not to mention my outfit isn't doing such a good job against the sun. I'd rather be inside."

Wiping her eyes, she leaned into him as they made the short walk to the Hawthorne. He wrapped her in an arm and kept it there until unlocking the door to the suite. Once inside, Marcelo began laying her things on the coffee table in front of the sofa.

"Are you all right?" he asked.

She nodded and sat on the edge of the sofa, then leaned forward to arrange the spell items in a certain order. "Truly, I am sorry, Marcelo. May we please just do the spell forthwith?"

"Of course. Several things are on your mind, having aged hundreds of years in what seemed like an instant of sleep. You lost someone close to you through violence, and it's not every day we wake up to a peculiar world full of strangers." He knelt on the opposite side of the coffee table. "How can I help with the magic?"

Sybil had expected some reproach. Instead, the boyish vampire looked at her with enthusiasm while awaiting instructions for the spell. She continued to deceive him, and another pang of guilt lowered her gaze as she pretended to study the items on the table.

"I saw some maps in yonder lobby," she said. "Can you bring one forth?"

"I collected some from the receptionist when I checked in." He went to a writing desk and retrieved a walking map for the Salem area and a bigger one of Massachusetts. "Salem has grown larger and more populated than the Salem Village you used to know. Massachusetts is also a state now instead of a colony. It will take a long time to explain America's history, but for now I'm certain you're anxious to locate your family."

Sybil widened her eyes at the charts. She had already been overwhelmed by the magnitude, sights, and sounds of everything around her. She desired to learn more about her modern environment, but Marcelo had been right about her greater need to focus on the current situation and magic.

"I shall fancy the history lesson on another day," she said. After a moment of studying the maps, she laid out the smaller one of Salem. "Years agone when I lost something on my property, I would sketch the layout of my cottage and the yard. A location spell would show forth yonder item on the drawing. Performing this magic on my home is simple, but on the entire city…or the state? My mind is distressed, I warrant. Truly, I am not certain I can do this."

"With your boosted powers, I believe you can," Marcelo stated. "Just be aware that you may not have any relatives in Salem at all, or even in Massachusetts. Current modes of travel can take people anywhere in the world, and rather quickly. People move to different places all the time. They find a new job, get bored with where they are, or simply want to start over. We may have to use a map of the entire country and narrow down the search from there."

Sybil realized this would be more difficult than anticipated, but she had to begin somewhere. "Let us commence in Salem. Perhaps luck shall be with us."

In a small iron cauldron, she crushed the petals of a forget-me-not, a reminder of those who executed Constance. She wrote the words *Those I Seek* on a scrap of paper and rolled it up tight, then bound it in black string. She gestured to the four brown candles, the color having properties used to locate lost things, and Marcelo lit them using a match. The burning candles were set around the spread map to represent the compass points.

Sybil ignited the scroll that held her written desire and dropped the flaming paper into the cauldron, then placed the lid. To stimulate her psychic power, she burned some acacia incense, then took several deep breaths to clear her mind.

In a state of active meditation, she poked her index finger using a needle Marcelo had cleaned and squeezed a few drops of blood onto the map of Salem.

Sybil then chanted, *"Compass points whose directions bind, reveal those that I may find. By blood, by ash, in centuries past, my true desire through time shall last."*

If she had been alone, her words, materials, and crafting would have been very different. However, she had to mask her real intention of vengeance and uphold Marcelo's belief that she sought her family line. Her method for this spell didn't represent her best effort, but not having a choice, the process would have to suffice.

Searching, the blood beads moved randomly around the chart, hesitating in some areas, then moving on. Sybil gasped when the drops split in half, then split again until over a dozen moved around. The blood drops finally settled across numerous neighborhoods. On the western side of Salem, one red bead glowed brightly. Its light pulsed like a tiny heart.

"There's so many," Marcelo said in wonder. "This is fantastic. Your family line branched out and settled here after all. But why is one drop glowing?"

"Yonder light represents a direct line to one of my siblings. Like a tree, several branches grow forth from the trunk, yet family blood can weaken as the branches spread. The stronger, pure bloodline always flows along the trunk and straight to the root." Sybil pointed at the illuminated blood, then glanced up at Marcelo. "I desire to meet this person. The other drops on the chart matter not."

Her pulse quickened in anticipation. Whose bloodline did she reveal? Was it Constable Daniel, or the court magistrate, Barton Acker? The other drops proved irrelevant; too many descendants populated the city. Sybil only cared about direct links to certain individuals.

The glowing blood represented her most concentrated anger, a target for her three-hundred-year retribution.

Marcelo tapped something on his phone, then showed Sybil the screen. "I brought up a map of Salem, and the glowing drop seems to have stopped over this house on Marlborough Road. That must be it."

"Truly wonderful, Marcelo. Let us attempt the map of Massachusetts. Curiosity overcomes me to see what occurs."

They prepared the table and cast the spell again, this time using the larger state map. The drops of blood danced across the chart and split like before. Not seeing any illuminated beads, Sybil was about to call this incantation a failure when two glowing drops finally settled over the city of Boston.

"Woo!" Marcelo cried, pumping his fist. "That was awesome. You have incredible skill, Sybil. Looks like you have more direct family lines in Boston."

Sybil grinned. "This is remarkable, I warrant, and I give you thanks for helping me. My body trembles in anxiety, but excitement overcomes me as well. I fancy a visit to yonder house in Salem, yet I ask that you to take me elsewhere first. Would it trouble you? I conceive traveling in daylight is uncomfortable for you, and dangerous."

"My carriage, and additional movie references, are at your service," Marcelo replied. "Where do you want to go?"

Sybil extinguished the candles and snuffed out the incense. She stood and walked to one of the windows, all of them curtained to protect Marcelo from the sun's rays. She peeked outside and gazed over the city, a deep sigh lifting her shoulders. "I wish to have a fair sight of where the witch hangings occurred. Does yonder place still stand?”

Marcelo did something on his phone, the tome of technology that amazed Sybil so much. She hadn’t forgotten his promise to buy her one.

“It does,” he said after a few moments. “It says here that for years, the site was thought to be Gallows Hill. However, a research team investigated documents from the period and performed some field work. The new location for the executions is Proctor’s Ledge, only a quarter mile from Gallows Hill.” He grabbed his protective clothing. “Ready to go?”

In the car, Sybil maintained a pensive silence until Marcelo stopped at a tome of technology store. It seemed he hadn’t forgotten his promise to buy her one, either. She waited in anticipation until he emerged with a new phone in hand. After he got in the car, she took the white object and hardly contained her exhilaration as she stared at the screen.

“Thank you so much, truly!” she said in delight. “Please teach me how to use this tome.”

“There are a million things to show you,” he said, clicking his seatbelt. “For now, I’ll demonstrate how we call each other. Just press that button, then look for my name. See it? Now press here…no, not that! This one.”

She pressed the indicated icon, then jumped when his phone buzzed loudly.

Marcelo held the device to his ear. “Hold your phone just like I am.”

Sybil copied his movement and pressed the new phone to the side of her head. “Hi!” his voice said in her ear, at the same time he spoke in front of her. “We can talk like this at any time, no matter the distance between us. Now let me initiate the call, and you answer just like I did."

Strange noises sounded from Sybil's phone. She pressed the button and held the device to her ear.

"ARE YOU PRESENT?" she hollered.

"Whoa! You don't have to scream. Just speak in a normal tone."

Sybil spoke, and Marcelo responded. Laughter gripped her and she shook, breathless until the merriment subsided. "Truly, I cannot believe that such wonderful things exist. This tome…I mean phone, and how people communicate is so remarkable. There is much to learn, I warrant."

"I'll show you the internet, the way I find information, later tonight." He started the car, and they rolled away from the store.

Sybil's joyous mood had darkened as Marcelo stopped next to a building called Walgreens. Behind the structure, she looked upon a tree-covered hill and a sharp pain abruptly drove through her chest. This was the place. Hundreds of years had elapsed here and the scenery changed, but she recognized the long path to the execution site—the same hill she had run up and watched Constance die.

Her breath shallow, she exited the car and followed Marcelo up the grassy incline. Her feet grew heavy and knees weak after each step. An ache formed around her temples, and she felt ill. She swayed, and Marcelo caught her just before she fell.

"Sybil, you don't have to do this," he said in concern. "Let's go back. You've been through enough already."

"I must go forth," she uttered in a feeble voice. Her stomach churned as memories of the frenzied mob and Minister Kendrick's frightening countenance assaulted her mind. "Constance…I need to see yonder."

Marcelo held her waist, and they continued. As her surroundings grew more familiar, it turned out she did the leading. By the time they reached the execution site, Sybil could no longer stand. She sank to her knees and cried into Marcelo's arms as he sat next to her.

Each tear added fuel to her fire, a raging inferno that could no longer be contained. Sybil would not rest until the descendants lay dead at her feet. With no one else to inflict her wrath on, she blamed the descendants and their prior generations for everything. The glowing blood drops proved that the ash marks from her centuries-old spell still existed. Therefore, the guilty parties remained at large.

She stood and gazed around the wooded area. Her temples pounded in anger when she spotted a smiling couple holding their phones up to take pictures of each other. Like in the Crow Haven Corner, these ignorant citizens traveled here to gawk and disrespect a site where innocent people had been murdered.

"Take me away forthwith," she told Marcelo. Her fists trembled. It would only take a flick of her fingers to incinerate the two visitors.

"I wish to go to yonder house, the dwelling on Marlborough Road," Sybil demanded after they entered the car.

"So soon?" Marcelo asked. "Sybil, you don't look well, and I think you should slow down. I can take you to lunch, and then we can rest for a while. I'll show you more of your phone."

"Please take me," she insisted, staring out the side window. "I want you to leave me there. I shall call you after my visit." She sensed him staring at the back of her head.

"Okay," he said after a few moments. "Take this before you go." He dug in a pocket and handed her some greenish papers bound in a metal clip. "This is modern money. Invite this person, and their family if they have one, out to lunch. You'll have a lot to discuss. Sybil, are you sure you don't want me to accompany you?"

"I am certain." She took the money and looked at it with mild interest. "Of a truth, you have done so much for me, Marcelo. Yet this is something I must endure alone. The experience shall help me adapt to this time and place."

"I just hope you're able to convince them you're a relative," he said. "It won't be easy, but you do have the history behind you. And an abundant amount of charm." Smiling, Marcelo leaned in and kissed her on the cheek.

Her heart skipped. She returned the smile and cupped the side of his face with a gnarled hand. His blanched, undead skin felt cool, though his vibrant green eyes blazed full of life.

"Charm is something you lack," she jested, "but your presence is tolerable."

He nodded. "Fair enough. Now let's get you to your family."

After driving across the town, Sybil's anxiety increased. Marcelo stopped the vehicle in front of a light gray, two-story home. A white railing surrounded the raised porch. He checked the map on his phone.

"This is it," he said. "Before I drive off, I'll wait to make sure someone is home."

Trembling, Sybil climbed out of the car and walked toward the house. She ascended a few steps until reaching the wooden porch, then rapped on the door. Throat dry, she swallowed when a blond woman opened the entrance. Sybil glanced back to Marcelo. He waved from the car, then drove away.

"May I help you?" the woman asked.

Branded by powerful magic, the descendants would not be able to see the ash marks on their hands—only Sybil had that privilege. However, this woman did not carry the mark on her flesh. Heavy disappointment crushed Sybil. She felt foolish and vulnerable standing on the porch. Had she committed an error during the location spell? Did Marcelo leave her at the wrong house?

"I am…I am not certain," Sybil replied.

"Stacy, who's at the door?" another woman's voice called from further inside the home. Footsteps approached. Wiping her hands on a towel, a brown-haired female appeared. "Oh, hello. I'm Elizabeth, and this is my neighbor, Stacy. Are you selling something today? We're kind of busy getting ready for our canvas and cocktail party."

Sybil barely heard a word. Ash stained the back of Elizabeth's right hand. The woman's ancestors had carried the mark through the generations, oblivious of its presence or meaning. Did Elizabeth come from one of the barbaric men who had dragged Constance up the hill? Or perhaps from the hangman himself?

In the end, Sybil only needed proof of the woman's guilt and she found it stamped on Elizabeth's hand. After sleeping for hundreds of years, the dark symbol had mocked Sybil in horrific nightmares. Rocks pelted her and split her skull. Her mother lay sprawled on the pier, drowning in her own blood. Constance writhed and choked at the end of a rope. Minister Kendrick and Barton Acker laughed. The cruel mob cheered. Black ash flew like rotten snow and poured into Sybil's mouth. It fed her endless sorrow, nourished her unlimited fury, and suffocated whatever remained of her soul.

Sybil did not observe a woman named Elizabeth standing there. Instead, Minister Kendrick sneered. Barton Acker shouted accusations. Constable Daniel tightened a noose.

No more suffering or tears. Today, Sybil's rage would be unleashed.

She extended her arm toward the neighbor, Stacy. Black smoke spewed from her hand just as it had in the restaurant. Stacy fell backwards in a deep sleep.

Elizabeth screamed. She tried to slam the door, but Sybil kicked out and blocked it. The woman scrambled into her living room and nearly tripped over an easel. Several of the stands had been set up, each with a blank canvas ready for paint. A bottle of wine and several glasses rested on a table.

In a panic, Elizabeth grabbed her phone from a chair and dropped it. She snatched it back up and frantic fingers pressed buttons. Sybil ran toward her and slapped the phone onto the carpet. She wrapped her fingers into Elizabeth's hair and grabbed tight, then thrust her other palm against the woman's chest.

A hot, white light glowed from Sybil's palm and absorbed into her victim's body. Elizabeth cried out and struggled. Soon her efforts waned as the spell drained her life force. Like a vampire drinking blood to survive, the witch siphoned years and vitality out of Elizabeth. The woman's energy flooded Sybil in a steady stream.

She closed her eyes in ecstasy and chanted. "*Your life to mine, the spirits unwind, a sacrifice is given. Release your soul and give unto me, for my will is truly driven.*"

She finished the spell, and Elizabeth collapsed on the floor. Glancing around, Sybil listened for any noise to ensure no one else lurked in the house. She walked toward the stairs, and an explosive ache ruptured in her chest. She staggered against the wall, then screamed when her skin burned as if on fire.

Sybil fell and writhed in excruciating pain as though a great beast chewed on her. Jagged teeth punctured her torso and ripped apart her limbs. She cried out in physical agony, but her mind sang in delight.

The spell had worked.

Her old, brittle bones hardened. Worn muscles and joints rejuvenated. Her baggy skin tightened, and the blemishes cleared. Renewed brown hair grew from her scalp and formed a thick, fluffy curtain. Invigorated blood pumped in a young heart, her organs fresh and healthy.

Breathing as if she had sprinted for a mile, Sybil stood and examined the smooth, supple skin on her hands and arms. She combed fingers through her straight brown hair and touched her soft face.

Giggling in excitement, she bounded up the stairs to look for a mirror. Finding one in the master bedroom, Sybil stripped off her clothes and inspected the lithe body of a teenager. Unlike the bent and shriveled body of before, her curves filled the correct places, a narrow waist and full breasts. Shapely legs and toned arms reflected the hard work of maintaining a colonial home in the seventeenth century.

Moving closer to the mirror, Sybil smiled at the light splash of freckles high on her cheeks. She stared into her brown eyes, the color of afternoon tea as her mother used to say. Her hair hung free and beautiful around bare shoulders.

Lowering her gaze, she moved her necklace aside and frowned at the pentagram scar branded into her chest. Her pentacle had glowed on the day of Constance's hanging, the result of Sybil's unexpected boost of magical power. Like the ash marks on those she hunted, the brand on her chest provided another reminder of more work to be done.

Sybil dressed and went downstairs. The women had not moved. She believed Stacy would eventually wake; however, Elizabeth's fate remained uncertain. Not concerned, Sybil stepped outside and walked down Marlborough Road. The sun felt exquisite on her young skin, her steps light and easy.

She burst forth in a run. After passing several houses, she drew stares from a couple trimming hedges on their lawn. Sybil didn't care. The sensation of being young again, powerful, and having just avenged Constance filled her with vigor.

She slowed after approaching a street called Highland Avenue. Spotting several eating and shopping establishments, Sybil crossed the street and entered a place with the peculiar name of IHOP. Not having any idea what to eat, she asked for a recommendation and the server produced a bacon crusted chicken breast alongside potatoes and white gravy.

Sybil cleaned her plate and guzzled a cold glass of peach mango juice. Astounded by the taste and quality of her meal, she imagined the food invigorated her as much as draining that woman's life had. Full and content, she called Marcelo and tried to explain her whereabouts.

"Yes, we finished eating and they returned home," she said into the phone. "'Twas an incredible experience I wish to share with you. Come hither, and I shall meet you outside."

Marcelo was sure to faint when he saw her! Excited to see his reaction, Sybil paid for the meal and stepped outdoors.

Chapter Eight

Undead Heart, Unrestrained Passion

Marcelo drove slowly through the IHOP parking lot, but he didn't see Sybil anywhere. He pulled around the back of the restaurant, searching. His phone rang, and he answered.

"Your carriage traveled past me!" Sybil laughed into his ear.

"What? I didn't see you."

"Seek the young girl by yonder restaurant sign." She disconnected the line.

Marcelo's head spun. What young girl? He had spotted a brown-haired beauty outside, but no way that could be Sybil. Had the witch pulled some sort of illusion spell?

He approached the entrance of the building and stopped the rented BMW in front of the girl. His eyes widened in shock, now noticing the same clothes the old version of Sybil had put on this morning. Except now a youthful, lively female stood inside the outfit.

Marcelo lowered the window, and the girl approached. She turned around in a circle and spread her arms, grinning.

"Am I a fair sight?" she asked. "Much better than an old hag?"

"I don't believe it," he said, dumbfounded at the change.

This was certainly not an illusion. How could this have happened? No minor ingredients and coffee table magic would produce such an outcome. Marcelo wanted to be happy for Sybil, but he couldn't help the wariness creeping under his skin.

Sybil walked around the car and sat inside. Marcelo stared and inspected her from head to toe.

"Amazing," he finally stated, quite a serious understatement but all he could utter. "Congratulations, Sybil. Did that house happen to have a fountain of youth in the backyard?"

"The people who dwell in yonder home are witches," she said as they drove away from the parking lot. "No surprise overcame me considering it is my family bloodline. I explained everything hitherto and showed forth my necklace. I then discovered my pentacle was not the only magical item passed down through the generations. Their great-grandmother, Elise, had talismans, potions, and a sundry of items she had kept years agone. We formed a family coven, bound by true blood, and performed an ancient spell using the heirlooms. Thus, my youth was restored, and I am forever in their debt."

"And they just abandoned you here at IHOP?" Marcelo asked.

Why couldn't he shake the skepticism? He wanted to smile at Sybil and share her joy, but the situation seemed too perfect. Having centuries of experience in the supernatural world, he knew nothing of this magnitude transpired easily.

Her face fell after his question, and a spike of guilt replaced his suspicion. "I'm sorry, Sybil. I didn't mean to sound doubtful. It's just…well, what the heck do I know about ancient witchcraft? I really am happy for you, and your smile in front of the restaurant spoke volumes about how you feel. If you're satisfied, then that's good enough for me."

"Thank you, Marcelo. I shall see them again, I warrant. But first it would please me to visit one of the places in Boston. Supposedly, I have more family yonder."

"We can do the spell again, this time with a city map instead of the state," he said. "That way we'll have a more accurate location."

Marcelo drove into the Hawthorne parking lot but didn't shut off the engine. "You know, I just realized you need new outfits. You can't go around looking like a young gal dressed in her momma's clothes. You need the latest fashion trends and the hottest styles for a rebellious teenager."

Sybil's eyes lit up beneath a wide smile. "Let us travel after dark. Truly, you ought not be out in the sun wrapped in protection. I wish for you to be relaxed and fancy an enjoyable time with me. I may give forth my hand unto yours, and I would desire to feel your skin, not a glove."

This moment provided another example of when Marcelo may have blushed, and his heart quickened. However, the lack of blood flow and a non-beating heart saved him from discomfort under the gaze of a beautiful girl.

"Maybe I don't want to hold yours," he said.

Laughing at the sour look on her face, he turned off the car and got out. They returned to the room and performed another location spell using a map of Boston to narrow down her family addresses in that city. Sybil's drop of blood split repeatedly, but she only focused on the two illuminated beads. One glob sat hovering over a zone in South Boston east of Highway 93, and the other drop slid to an area on Seaver Street east of the Franklin Park Zoo.

Marcelo spent the afternoon teaching Sybil how to use her new smartphone. Her fascination over the device, combined with an unrelenting fervor to learn, made her a semi-pro after a couple hours. She cherished selfies, became enthralled with the map function, and couldn't believe just how much information existed in the world.

Afterwards, he spoke a great deal about the history she had missed as well as modern events. He explained the development of America following the Colonies, globalization, commerce, wars, and other topics that may have bored a student, but Sybil drew it all in like a sponge. Her questions pelted him from every angle, but he smiled at her enthusiasm and explained everything as best he could.

After sundown, they drove to Northshore Mall in Peabody. He barely kept up as she floated from store to store, falling in love with clothes suitable for someone her age. She tried on everything, and of course, made him pass judgment for every outfit.

Marcelo adored her exuberant spirit and resilient character. Born again with a second chance at life, Sybil had overcome horrendous adversity and trauma to grow and adapt in her new world. Alone, lost, and plagued by an unknown danger, she embraced the challenge and so far, had surpassed her trials. Much work remained to discover why he had been led to Sybil, not to mention avoiding or defeating Minister Kendrick. But Marcelo knew she would be all right, and he would never leave her side.

Loaded with a dozen bags, Marcelo and Sybil returned to the car after she devoured a burger and fries at the food court. She wore a new outfit of stretch faded skinny jeans, topped by a flowing black, elbow-sleeve tunic tee. She loved the white Converse All-Star Chuck Taylor's adorning her feet.

Before he could start the engine, she tapped something into her phone and showed him the screen. "Let us travel here next."

Stunned, Marcelo stared as he saw the display. "That's a blood studio. Why do you want to go there?"

"You must break your fast, Mister Vampire," she said casually. "You watched me consume that hamburger and fries. Forthwith, it is my turn to observe you."

"I'm fine. Sustenance is not something I need right now. Besides, it's just…I don't know. It would be weird taking you there."

"Does shyness about being an undead overcome you? It seems odd to behave in this manner. Come, let us travel yonder. It would please me very much."

Marcelo didn't know why Sybil's presence at a blood studio disturbed him. Drinking blood represented his nature, and he had done it several times in front of friends at other studios, or at someone's party, even in his home. But things felt different with Sybil. Maybe he didn't want her to witness him in his most primal, feral state.

Behind the calm, controlled feeding process lurked a savage demon yearning to tear open necks and arteries. Long ago, Marcelo had quelled those impulses, yet a demonic soul truly possessed him in place of his human one. His memories and emotions remained, but the monster part of him always required blood—the beast *demanded* it, something Marcelo could never evade. Having Sybil watch him at his worst, lowest moment was not something he desired to share with her.

But you have shared it with so many others, the demon inside Marcelo mocked. *Like with those dead people whose throats you ripped out back in the old days. Before society pacified you in disgrace!*

Marcelo closed his eyes and willed the parasitic monster to shut up.

"Your mind seems distressed," Sybil observed. "Do not avoid this lest you believe I shall gaze upon you differently, Marcelo. Fear not. After everything we have striven for, never would I leave you in this matter. Remember, we are linked by a mysterious force. Thus, I am part of your life and I wish to experience this with you."

In the hotel, Sybil had not held back when she recounted her story. Her detailed narrative, endless tears, and powerful emotions had sent Marcelo back in time to witness her life of fear and hardship. She had given him a piece of her broken heart, and in that moment, he realized just how potent the bond stood between them. What he shared with Sybil proved to be stronger than a taunting demon, and he would not allow the beast inside to destroy that trust.

"You're right, I'm stuck with you," he finally said. "And you're stuck with me." He smiled at her, and she grasped his outstretched hand. "Let's head to the blood studio."

The Vampire's Cauldron, a charming and suitable name given the club's mixed theme of vampire and witch, sat on a small peninsula between the North River and Collins Cove. Holding her hand, Marcelo led Sybil into the lively establishment. Patrons packed a dance floor as the DJ spun a feet-moving remix of Ellie Goulding's "On My Mind." Many vibrant Halloween decoration including fog, neon spider webs, and animated creatures added to the cool atmosphere.

"This is wonderful!" Sybil yelled over the noise. "Thank you for bringing me hither." Her energetic eyes matched her huge grin. She looked everywhere, at the people-filled tables, the hanging ornaments, and the boisterous dance floor.

"Welcome," a man said as he approached. "My name is Nathan, and I hope you both are well this evening. Do you have a reservation? If not, I'm afraid the wait time is one hour."

Marcelo figured they could just return later. "We don't have—"

"We do," Sybil jumped in. "For table seven, I warrant. Sybil and Marcelo."

Marcelo gaped at her in surprise. "When did you make a reservation?"

"'Twas while I changed clothes at the large stores…the mall," she answered. "I reserved a table using the tome…the smartphone. But of a truth, I did not have the courage to ask you to bring me forth.

Anticipation filled my heart all night, thus I made the reservation to be prepared."

"You are a big jar of secrets, witch," Marcelo replied, smiling. "Lucky for you I agreed to come."

"I have you down," the attendant said after checking his tablet. "May I please see your ID, Mr. Flores?" He took Marcelo's driver's license. "All blood studios are connected across the country, and I see you are registered in the system." Nathan nodded and returned the ID. "Thank you. This way, please."

Marcelo exchanged nods with three other vampires seated at booths and tables. Humans clustered around the undead to engage in spirited conversation over drinks or leaned back quietly during feedings. Nurses in crisp uniforms and Halloween painted faces attended their stations.

In a private booth, Marcelo scooted onto a velvet loveseat next to Sybil. Unexpectedly nervous, he glanced around, waiting for the assigned nurse and the client blood donor to appear.

"Would it please you to show me some modern dancing afterwards?" Sybil asked. "It looks strange and awkward, but enjoyable, I warrant."

"Yeah, I'd love to dance with you. However, looking strange and awkward on the dance floor is normal for me."

"Truly, I shall appear much worse," she said, standing from the loveseat. "I shall go forth to search for the privy."

The nurse or the client still hadn't appeared by the time Sybil returned. She slid back into the seat and snuggled against Marcelo.

With a face painted like Spiderman, the nurse, Jeremy, finally approached while pushing a tray table of sterilized gear.

"Good evening," he said to Marcelo, glancing over a tablet. "I apologize for the delay." He then faced Sybil. "Would you be Sybil R. Cotterill, young lady?"

"I am," she replied.

"Thank you for registering with the Vampire's Cauldron," Jeremy continued. "I see in our records this is your first time. Are you ready?"

Sybil held out her arm, and the nurse began to prepare it.

Marcelo stiffened as though ice water splashed his body. If he had had an active heart, it would have burst from shock. "What are you doing? This isn't possible. I won't allow it!"

Sybil leaned in to speak softly in his ear. "The nurse speaks true, I am registered. After finding Nathan yonder, it only took the power of suggestion and a little spell to sign up without an ID. Relax, dear vampire. Do not be troubled."

Marcelo didn't know what bothered him the most—that Sybil had manipulated someone with her magic to register illegally, or the thought of drinking the blood of someone he cared about so much. Just bringing her here had been enough of an emotional challenge. Now he faced the prospect of feeding on her.

The preparations finished, and the nurse stepped away. Marcelo started to rise from the sofa, but Sybil latched onto his arm.

"I can't do this," he told her. "I was fine with having you watch, but to feed on you…"

She scooted closer and molded her warm body against his. Her soft lips brushed his ear when she whispered, and her breath sent a bolt of lightning down his spine that made him shiver. "I wish to do this, Marcelo. I cannot conceive of where I would be without you, and never could I repay you for your kindness and protection. Truly, this is the very least I can do. Please, allow me forthwith to share more of my life with you."

Marcelo turned to face her. The expressive, light brown eyes of a young girl who had experienced unbearable hardship stared into his. The dusting of freckles rode high on her cheeks, unpainted lips rosy and full. Her skin smelled of blossoms over a dew-specked field, her hair a sweet aroma of spring breeze and honey.

Sybil grasped the drinking tube and brought it to his lips. "Be with me," she said, then leaned into his chest and closed her eyes.

Marcelo's mind and emotions warred. This seemed wrong, a break of trust and a violation of friendship. Yet the demon soul screamed for blood. Marcelo smelled hers, and it dizzied him like an intoxicating perfume. Sybil's heart thundered over the boom of the music. Her wrist and neck pulsed in rhythm.

The music changed, and "Heathens" by Twenty One Pilots spilled out of the speakers. Entranced by Sybil's request and overpowered by her very being, Marcelo moved as if in a dream. The drinking tube slid between his lips, and her blood poured into his mouth.

The Vampire's Cauldron disappeared, as did the people and everything else. Only Marcelo and Sybil existed, forever bound by the act of sharing part of her life and soul. Her blood ran hot, fresh, and invigorating over his tongue. Chills raced over his skin. His toes curled and fingers dug into her shoulders. He drew her closer and lost himself in her aura, her scent, her soft texture as she moaned against his neck.

Marcelo swallowed her memories and pain. He shared in her laughter, love, and misery when it struck over the course of her life. He experienced Sybil at her worst and witnessed the girl at her best. He bathed in her omnipresent soul and it burned, blinded, and consumed him in return.

"Do not ever leave me," she whispered. "I need you to understand."

Marcelo removed the tube and set it aside. "I won't leave you, not ever," he murmured, running his fingers through her hair. Abandoning Sybil would never happen, but what did she mean by needing him to understand?

The nurse stepped back near the booth. "I'm sorry, time is up."

Their blissful moment ended, and the club jumped back to life. Music pumped, and conversation roared. Jeremy cleaned Sybil's arm and removed the equipment, then set down a plate of cookies and juice.

"Enjoy the rest of your evening," he said before departing.

Sybil consumed the treats, then leapt up and pulled Marcelo's hand. "Dancing! You promised."

Out on the dance floor, Marcelo couldn't stop smiling. Sybil shook, twirled, and flailed her arms to the music. She adapted nicely to the simple club-style of dancing, nothing fancy required. Before he knew it, the final song for the night played and last calls for drinks announced.

They drove back to the Hawthorne in silence. The mesmerizing effects of the evening still buzzed in Marcelo's head. The taste of Sybil's blood remained. Her scent lingered on his clothes. He glanced at her. As she gazed out into the night, a tiny smile curved her lips, her eyes large and pensive.

In the hotel room, Marcelo's keys barely hit the desk when Sybil stood before him, her hands on his chest. Her gaze burned into his, and a powerful connection similar to the blood bond shivered his spine. He lost himself in her eyes that had seen so much life and tragedy. She seemed on the verge of tears, and he only desired to bring her joy and respite. Her expression turned distant and difficult to read, her silence a commanding roar that blasted him with unrestrained emotion.

Sybil slowly moved forward and wrapped her arms around his neck. He drew her heated body against his and slid a hand against her back in gentle strokes. With his preternatural senses, he felt her heart crash against his chest. The rich vibrations smothered him in *life*.

She possessed an irresistible force. The enigma surrounding her presence and special character enticed him. Marcelo cupped her face and ran the pad of a thumb over her lips. Captivated by her scent, he leaned forward and kissed her softly. She welcomed the gesture and returned the kiss in greater intensity.

After a moment they pulled back and locked eyes. Sybil's cheeks flushed, and her breath grew rapid. Marcelo searched her gaze for an answer as to where this may lead. Did they have time for a relationship while trying to figure out why they had been brought together in the first place? Someone undoubtedly watched from afar and had pulled his and Sybil's strings. How much danger were they in?

She took a tentative step away and closed her eyes. Her head lowered and shoulders sagged. Her look and posture revealed utter exhaustion, but more than just physical. Something troubled her as if a mental weight crushed her spirit.

Do not ever leave me. I need you to understand.

Sybil's words from the blood studio crept into Marcelo's head. She had whispered that in a moment of passion. Pleasantly drugged by his experience with her, he hadn't thought too much about what she had said until now.

Her strange behavior worried Marcelo as she trembled. "Sybil, sweetheart, what's the matter? Please talk to me."

She opened her eyes and reached for his hand. "Lay down with me, Marcelo. Please hold me until I fall asleep."

Sybil dressed for bed and waited for Marcelo in the room. He slipped under the covers, and she snuggled against his body. Sleep conquered her in only a few moments. He held her close and bathed in her heat. The steady thunder of her heart soothed him. Sometimes her grip tightened, and she mumbled or cried out in agitated dreams.

A fierce protectiveness for her overcame him. He cared a great deal for the witch, and his simple agreement to work together had developed into something more. They had shared loss through multiple lifetimes, endured trauma, and both had tried to find a place in the world while sidelined by society.

Sybil jerked again as something haunted her. Tears wet her cheeks. Marcelo kissed the top of her head, and whispered, "You have suffered too long, my dear. I am here for you, always."

Chapter Nine

Inca Empire, 1532

High in the mountains of the Cuzco region, the great Inca city of Machu Picchu overlooked the Sacred Valley. Thick gray clouds hovered, and cold rain pounded Cauac's home in the residential district as he worked inside a ritual chamber. The water roared off the angled, thatched roof and splashed against the walls built from granite blocks.

On the dusty floor lay the horrid, broken body of a dead demon he had just summoned. Or rather, failed to summon in the correct manner.

Irritated at the botched ritual, Cauac paced the area, his arms crossed. The blood of a sacrificed llama shone wet on a large stone block. Mixed herbs and crushed powder used for magic sat in various bowls. A crackling fire that served as a portal for the demon to step through blazed in the center of the room.

In anger, Cauac kicked the lifeless demon. "Why did my spell not work?" he shouted in Quechua. "You're supposed to be alive and at my command."

Sharp protrusions speckled the demon's gray, hairy back. A long snout extended beneath three closed eyes, and curved teeth filled a wide maw. The lower half of its body had been crushed and twisted when the portal collapsed during the summoning. Had Cauac not used enough blood? Did he erroneously utter the incantation, or use the wrong herbs?

The door burst open. Illapa, the priest of Inti Watana, the Temple of the Sun, strode into the ritual chamber. Belted with colored cords, a ceremonial knee-length tunic adorned by divine symbols swished around his legs. A jeweled headdress covered his scalp and the sides of his face. He recoiled at the bloody sight and covered his nose against the vile smell Cauac had long gotten used to.

"This is disgusting, Cauac, and an abomination to our culture," Illapa chided. "The foreign invaders from across the ocean are marching closer to Machu Picchu every day, and you waste your time in here playing with malevolent creatures. You are a layqa, a spellcrafter and spiritual healer of our people. Aren't you going to do anything to save our city?"

"I know what I am, priest," Cauac muttered. "My name means He Who Guards, and that is precisely what I've been doing. These demons will fight for the Inca under my command. My creatures will drive out the invaders, unlike Inti, your useless sun god. Our people are being slaughtered by these Conquistadors. And where is the all-powerful Inti? He does nothing while the Inca suffer! We will be wiped out of history, Illapa. But not if I can master this portal and bring forth the demon horde."

"Blasphemy!" Illapa cried. "You turned your back on our gods, Cauac. Summoning dark beings is not our way. The sun deity is surely angered, and you will burn in his light."

"Inti will fear me when I succeed," Cauac retorted. "You should be grateful, priest. All the Inca will look to me as their new god, a flesh and blood layqa at the pinnacle of Machu Picchu."

"You speak madness," Illapa replied as he backed toward the doorway. "The people will put an end to your sacrilege, if not the great Inti himself." The priest turned and strode out.

Over the next several days, Cauac explored every corner of the mountain and rainforest in search of stronger ingredients for his dark magic. He collected tiny, poisonous frogs and toxic mushrooms he had never used before. He even bewitched a precious jaguar and brought it to his home like a pet. After slaughtering the animal, he burned its pelt on the fire and used its blood to inscribe glyphs on the stone altar.

Night fell and Cauac prepared the summoning ritual. He built the fire high and threw a potion onto the flames. The fire hissed and lashed out as if to pull him into the inferno. Raising his arms, he cried out the incantation. *"I cast away the gods of old and raise the new from deep, open wide the portal from nether, and let my enemies weep! My will, my desire, no foe can withstand, come forth the demon army, howling at my command!"*

The roaring flames turned the color of blood. A terrifying scream from within the fire vibrated the stone walls and thatch roof. The floor trembled and a reddish, skinless arm thrust out of the blaze. Sinew, muscle, and veins snaked along the gleaming limb. A cloven hoof and leg stripped of skin followed, a tremendous boom echoing when the hoof stepped down. A bald, veiny head emerged wearing an inhuman face that lacked a nose. The demon's entire body finally moved through the portal. Gray worms squirmed on its torso. No flesh covered its midsection; decayed intestines and organs rotted in the air.

Cauac looked up at the towering monster, its head as high as the walls. Black eyes like polished obsidian gleamed in the firelight.

"Welcome, Nala'thelx!" Cauac exclaimed. "Bid the rest of your soldiers to appear and purge the realm of my enemies."

"Fool human," Nala'thelx growled. "Only by luck do you have the strength to control me. I am bound by your magic, but at the slightest error on your part, I will devour your insides!"

Cauac did not fear this demon. He had the courage and skill to defy the all-powerful sun god, Inti, so this monster posed no threat. Confidence surged after his spell's success. A lust for more power and control burst in each beat of his heart.

"Stop wasting time," he told Nala'thelx. "My era of supremacy has arrived."

The demon bellowed and spat onto the fire. The flames grew and danced toward the ceiling. A multitude of screams discharged from the blaze and a torrent of lesser demons rushed out of the portal.

The three-eyed, snarling gray foot soldiers resembled the spiked and hairy demon that had been killed in Cauac's previous attempt to open the gateway. The creatures lumbered outside into the night, followed by Nala'thelx as he yelled at them in a demonic tongue.

Cauac watched the train of otherworldly beasts scamper in the moonlight. Instead of leaving Machu Picchu and descending the mountain towards the Conquistador camps, the demons smashed in doors and attacked Incas in their beds. Terrified screams and frenzied shouts erupted from the city. Some residents escaped their homes only to be tackled and ripped apart in the plaza.

Cauac froze at the slaughter of his people. His spell had backfired…or had it? He had called on the demons to defeat his opponents, to carry out his will.

Abrupt laughter shook him as he realized the irony. His spell did not go wrong—this was exactly what his inmost desire had requested. The Inca priests and the people who worshipped Inti posed the greatest obstacle to achieving his status as a ruler having deity-like power.

Illapa had not been the only one to criticize Cauac and doubt his abilities. For years, the citizens had mocked his progress and ridiculed his aspirations. The people of Machu Picchu now experienced his true purpose and potential. Let the old Inca gods witness the rise of Cauac!

An explosion reverberated across the sky, and an enormous light blasted down from the heavens. The radiance collected into a massive ball and floated down to the city. The demon soldiers howled and tried to run, but the bright phenomenon burned them to ash using dazzling rays of light. Only Nala'thelx escaped. His body ablaze and trailing smoke, the beast ran to the edge of the bastion and leapt off the mountain in a thunderous roar.

"Cauac!" a voice boomed from the spherical light. "Your wicked and corrupt ways are at an end. Stand before me and be judged."

Terror rooted Cauac to the path. The great sun god had manifested to save the Inca after all, but not from the Conquistadors. Seeing Inti after a year without so much as a divine whisper, Cauac's initial fright dwindled until only anger remained. His frustration burst in a torrent.

"And what is my punishment, you inattentive god?" Cauac shouted. "Over the years I've done nothing but try to help the Inca. I've worshipped you, prayed, and demonstrated my devotion. Yet I cannot even heal a sick child because of your absence. What does that say about you? You are the one that failed, Inti!"

"I did not fail, you did," the sun god's voice rumbled from the glow. "Long has your heart dwelled in darkness where not even my light could penetrate. Your selfish quest for greater power turned me away. The ruined crops and sick children suffered through no one's fault but your own. And now you manipulate wicked, dangerous creatures to prove your significance. These demons attacked your own people, proof that your black heart cares for no one except yourself."

"I've done more than you ever could, you useless deity!" Cauac screamed. "One day I will be greater than the gods, and the blackness in my heart will smother the world forever."

"You have blasphemed against and defiled the gods, the creators who established the Inca upon the earth," Inti responded. "Cauac, He Who Guards, is no more. I strip the name from your flesh—you are now called Umaq, The Betrayer. See what you have done and witness it not again."

Intense pain flared in Umaq's eyes. He cried out and fell to his knees, blind and chastised by Inti. Lost in the dark, he sensed the massive presence in the light rise and vanish into the heavens.

Hands pressed over his eyes, Umaq writhed in agony and sobbed into the dirt. He crawled down the path to try and reach his home. Footsteps approached and several hands seized him. Insults and dirt pelted him. The Inca survivors shouted into his face, but only blackness swam in his vision.

The people tossed The Betrayer off the side of the mountain. Umaq bounced and rolled down the slick embankment. Cuts and bruises peppered his skin. The fall seemed endless until a final crash left him stunned and breathless. Rain started anew and moisture washed over his broken body and mud-caked face.

"Nala'thelx," he called weakly. "Come to me, my demon. My vengeance has only begun. Together we will summon Inti and cast him down upon the mountain. I will blot out his light and darken the sun, just as he has shadowed my sight. I will turn to the netherworld and raise a new army of spite. Hear me, malicious gods of the underworld! I will shatter the walls between our realms and release your filth into this cursed world."

Fighting to remain conscious, Umaq detected strong arms lifting him. A rotten stench made him gag. Cold worms wriggled on his arms and legs as someone carried him away.

Nala'thelx had returned. The demon proved to be resilient and loyal. Umaq smiled. His greatest work had yet to be done. One day the world would bend knee to his ascension…and not even Inti could stop him.

Chapter Ten

Salem, Massachusetts - Present Day

"Umaq! Umaq!" cried Sebas, a rare species of yellow-tailed woolly monkey found only in the Peruvian Andes. Covered in fluffy brown fur and sporting a gray mouth and nose, the clever primate crouched on the second story windowsill of Kendrick's home. "The vampire and the witch are growing closer, just as you predicted."

Constructed in the 1800s, Kendrick's thirty-seven hundred square foot house sat on Bridge Street north of the Salem Witch Museum. Seated at a desk in the spacious study, he yanked off his glasses and slammed the laptop shut in exasperation. "I told you not to call me Umaq. I go by Kendrick and have so for centuries."

Sebas leapt from the windowsill onto a couch. The monkey acted as Kendrick's familiar, an attendant spirit in the form of an animal used to assist with spellcrafting and other duties.

"Yes! Yes!" said the primate. "But you can never erase your true name, Umaq. Inti has branded you with it forever."

Kendrick stood so fast his chair nearly toppled over. "Enough of that nonsense, Sebas! The sun god does not control who I am."

He moved to the mirror hanging on a wall between two large bookcases and squinted at his slightly blurred reflection. Centuries ago, Inti had ripped out his sight and left him with ugly yellow stains for eyes, but Nala'thelx had used demonic energy to restore most of Kendrick's vision. He would never see like he did before, but anything other than total blindness became a true gift.

"My prediction of Sybil and Marcelo growing close did not require magic or coercion," said Kendrick. "The witch's pentacle and my note in the undead's car had set everything in motion. Those two are alike in many ways and share a history as supernatural beings. The powerful witch restoring her youth was only a matter of time, which led to an expected attraction between the pair."

"So now Marcelo will turn Sybil into a vampire on his own?" Sebas asked. The monkey yanked a pillow from the couch and threw it across the room.

Kendrick picked up the pillow, fluffed it, then returned it to the couch. "On his own? I'm afraid not. That action will require difficult, costly, and time-consuming magic. I'll have to wait until the right moment to manipulate the demon soul buried inside Marcelo. Once the dark entity is under my control, I will force Marcelo to turn the witch."

Sebas jumped onto the desk and began chewing on the power supply cord for the laptop. "Demonic energy will then pass to the witch, and she will fall under your command," the monkey mumbled around the cord. "You will have a powerful witch-demon as your ally."

"After hundreds of years of sleeping, Sybil's abilities are at their peak. If all goes as planned, she will be my strongest and most successful experiment yet." Kendrick jerked the cable out of Sebas' mouth. "I can't believe I chose a primate as my familiar. You're too much trouble!"

"Trouble! Trouble! But very crafty and skilled, Umaq."

"Yes, you are, which is why I haven't squashed you yet." Kendrick moved to the window and put on his glasses. His vision improved a bit more, but he still couldn't fully enjoy what he imagined to be a gorgeous view.

"My army is increasing, Sebas. For centuries, I have experimented using demonic energies and mastered dark magic. With Sybil at the head of my troops, even Inti wouldn't dare stand against me. Soon I'll have enough power to open the ancient portals at Machu Picchu, effectively uniting this realm and the demon one. Afterwards, my revenge against the old sun god and my establishment as this world's ruler will finally come to pass."

Sebas bounced on the desk. "Revenge! How can I help?"

"Continue spying on the witch and vampire while I collect some materials for the spell to control Marcelo. Contact me if anything significant occurs."

Kendrick left his house and spent the rest of the day purchasing lesser ingredients for the incantation. Taking advantage of Salem's infatuation with witches, the modern era made it easy to acquire what he needed. In the various witch-themed stores, the employees were always friendly and eager to assist. However, the real dirty work would arrive at nightfall. The most difficult materials required for the spell might cost him his life.

Day faded and night blackened the sky. After hopping in his car, Kendrick pulled up to Harmony Grove Cemetery and adjusted his glasses before stepping out. His vision grew worse at night, which made this type of work dangerous. Hiking a small backpack over a shoulder, he walked into the shadowed graveyard and began searching for his target—a ghoul.

Kendrick moved between headstones, pausing every now and then to listen. Tall, angelic statues stood watch over some graves. In other areas, decorated mausoleums having carved friezes, Roman-style pillars, and etched marble steps housed the wealthier deceased. Several tree branches snaked overhead, the stars visible between patches of leaves.

A loud crunch froze him. Tensed and listening, a snap like a breaking branch popped to his right. Moving in a cautious crouch, he slid between two above-ground lawn crypts and hid in the shadows.

Ahead, a grotesque ghoul shoved a flesh-coated bone between its sharp teeth. It chomped down, and the bone cracked in half. Savoring its meal, the creature plunged its arm into the torn-up soil in front of a headstone. It pulled out a leg from a recently buried body the monster had freed from the underground casket.

Sporting a hunched back, the ghoul crouched using long, spindly limbs coated in a thin layer of diseased, bluish skin. Solid white eyes shone in a nasty, snarling face that resembled a bat. Large, pointed ears protruded from the sides of its head. Elongated fingers stripped flesh from the bone, the pieces promptly thrown into its wide mouth. Glistening drool stretched from its lips as it chewed.

Kendrick gestured toward a large tree. A branch creaked as it bent down to impale the ghoul through its back. The creature heard the noise and leapt out of the way. It then sniffed the air and charged on all fours.

Cursing, Kendrick rubbed his palms together and fire ignited on his hands. He thrust out his arms and launched a jet of flame towards the ghoul. The monster shrieked and ran through the inferno, its filthy nails slashing. Four parallel gashes ripped open Kendrick's coat and skin. He hollered in pain, then reached down and yanked off his belt to throw at the beast. The leather strap stretched and thickened into a tough cord as it sailed. On fire, the ghoul howled and collapsed when the binding wrapped its torso and legs.

Kendrick grimaced in agony and removed a hammer from the backpack. He ran toward the corpse-eater and smashed the tool on its head over and over until the creature stopped moving. The flame over its body slowly diminished, leaving behind a horrid stench.

Panting, Kendrick removed his shredded coat and inspected the bleeding wounds over his belly. Hands trembled as he rummaged in the pack and removed the herb-soaked poultices he crafted earlier for emergencies. He applied the compresses and hissed at the sting, but knew the strong medicine would perform its function and heal.

Using the claw end of the hammer, he worked the tool on the ghoul's face until its jawbone snapped off. He then plopped the jaw into a plastic bag and put everything away.

A bright light suddenly shone on him. An alarmed voice shouted, "What in the…holy hell! You there, freeze!"

Kendrick squinted against the flashlight and saw a police officer holding a gun. He stood in a wince and smiled. "Good evening, officer. Is there a problem?"

"We received a call about a disturbance in Harmony Grove," the uniformed man said. "I'm pretty sure I've found it. This activity coincides with the calls we've been getting about demon and monster sightings around Salem. Now place your bag on the ground, and turn around with your hands up!"

"Demon sightings?" Kendrick asked, holding a smile. "Oh, that would be my fault as well. Those are my soldiers, you see. Most of them are dormant and in hiding. But occasionally, one gets agitated or bored, and will surface."

The officer grabbed the radio handset attached to his shoulder. "Unit twelve, requesting back-up at Harmony Grove."

Kendrick laughed. "You'll be dead before your partners arrive. Unless you turn around and leave while forgetting everything you saw."

"Get your hands in the air!" the cop shouted. "I won't tell you again."

Kendrick clucked his tongue. "Pity. I was kind enough to give you a chance, which is unusual for me. Too bad you wasted it."

He lifted his eyes toward a nearby tree. A branch groaned and swept down like before, this time striking the cop through his back. The man screamed, and his gun fell onto the grass. The tree lifted the impaled body, and soon the officer stopped struggling.

"Rest in peace," Kendrick said as he hurried away from Harmony Grove.

Back home, he entered the kitchen and stripped off his bloody coat and shirt. He checked the poultices, then dabbed at the areas with an alcohol-soaked cloth. Finished, he grabbed the backpack and headed for his workshop.

During remodeling and modernization of the old house, some walls had been knocked down to create a huge, enclosed area for his spell-work. Lights snapped on as he stepped into the workshop. A combination of the newest computers and the oldest tomes and scrolls filled desks and shelves. A large wooden table carved with symbols sat in the center of the room. Jars, herbs, candles, spell books, and various other items for magic littered the surface. Cabinets stuffed with personal items, tools, blade weapons, and rare mystical artifacts lined the walls.

A growl sounded from a corner. The powerful demon, Nala'thelx, stepped forward on cloven hooves and towered over Kendrick. Pulsing veins snaked over the demon's skinless body, his limbs and torso red with corded muscle and sinew. Gray worms fell from his chest and plopped onto the floor. Like pieces of coal, black eyes in a nose-less face stared down in rage.

"Umaq!" Nala'thelx rumbled. "I will not remain here a prisoner. This is humiliating. Why do I have to keep hiding?"

Kendrick set down the backpack and took out the ghoul's jawbone. "I'm having enough difficulty keeping the lesser demons hidden. Your overwhelming presence in Salem will only attract unwanted attention and put my operation in jeopardy. However, I did let you out yesterday for a very specific task. Were you successful?"

Nala'thelx pulled a silver-plated box from a shelf and laid it on the table. Celtic runes and Egyptian hieroglyphs covered each side.

Kendrick approached the box and passed a hand over it. His palm grew warm, and goosebumps rose on his skin.

"A child's soul," he said. "Well done, Nala. How did you acquire it?"

"I hunted at the children's hospital and found the soul roaming the grounds," the demon answered. "This little boy had refused to cross over after succumbing to illness the night before. Now he's just a simple tool for your spell."

"Your task sounded much easier than mine. A ghoul nearly ripped open my guts tonight." Kendrick placed the rotting jaw next to the silver box.

"You risk everything," Nala'thelx warned. "Are you certain you can control Marcelo? He is not a demon from the netherworld, like I am."

"You are right, but he possesses the soul of a demon."

An odd expression passed over Nala'thelx's hideous face. "How is that possible? Vampires don't have souls."

"True, but Marcelo is a very unique creature," Kendrick began. "He isn't simply a blood-sucking, animated corpse lacking a soul. A demonic spirit lives inside him, and with that, I can control Marcelo. When he turns Sybil into an undead, some of that demonic energy will pass on to her, also making her susceptible to my influence."

"I never imagined such a creature could exist," the demon expressed. "So Marcelo is not a vampire in the traditional sense? As in, one bitten and created by another?"

"Correct, my veiny and wormed accomplice," Kendrick answered. "Another vampire did not sire him, to use a cliché term. But he was indeed created…by yours truly. A failed experiment in my early days, as I didn't account for his human mind and emotions remaining intact. Unlike you and other live demons, Marcelo is impossible to command without extensive time and preparation. Compelling him to turn Sybil won't be easy, but the act is well within my ability."

Nala'thelx gestured toward Kendrick's injuries. "That's if you don't die in the process, you weak human. But speaking of time and preparation, what about the witches from the Wyman Woods coven? Have they brought you the remaining ingredient, the wood sprite?"

"Not yet, but I do trust them," Kendrick stated. "Those witches desire my ascension just as much as I do. They crave recognition and power like in the ancient days, and I can give that to them. Between my demon army and my witch allies, nothing can stop us, Nala. And soon your hiding days will be over. You will rule by my side when the demon world and this one unite."

Nala'thelx raised his skinless head and bellowed so loud the walls of the room shook.

"I will feast on human misery and burn all who oppose me," the demon avowed. "No more cowering in the nether and in-between worlds. The time of my kin has come at last!"

Kendrick, better known as Umaq, smiled. The old god Inti had branded him as The Betrayer. What better way to live up to his name by destroying the world…and making humanity suffer.

Chapter Eleven

Undead Hearts Bleed Too

In Boston, Marcelo and Sybil had checked into the Eliot Hotel, a luxurious establishment decorated in old world European style with the benefits of modern comfort and technology. According to the website Marcelo had read, the hotel sat in the Back Bay neighborhood close to Boston's famous art galleries, cultural attractions, and designer shops at Copley Place and Newbury Street. He looked forward to sightseeing and taking Sybil shopping.

Boston was less than an hour away from Salem, and during the drive Marcelo had told Sybil more about the modern world. Arriving in the evening, they dined in the hotel restaurant called Uni, where Sybil thoroughly enjoyed a bowl of Japanese noodle soup. Afterwards, they hopped in the BMW and headed for the address on Seaver Street, just east of the Franklin Park Zoo.

"Are you all right?" Marcelo asked on the way. "You're rather quiet after having so much to say during dinner."

Sybil smiled, yet the emotion in her eyes did not match her facial expression. "Fear not, I believe only fatigue ails me. This whole affair about finding family is taxing. Hitherto I should be happy, like I was in Salem, but my heart is nervous about this voyage to Boston."

"If it makes you feel better, I can go with you this time. I'm not sure if these people want a vampire in their house, but I can just wait outside by the curb."

"No," she responded a bit loudly. "I mean, as in Salem, it behooves me to do this alone. I shall call you when I am ready for your carriage…your car."

"Ok. No worries."

Marcelo pulled up to a wood-slatted home with red trim. Large trees flanked the structure, and a balcony overlooked the street. Sybil leaned toward him, and he kissed her glossed, watermelon-flavored lips. Premiere by Gucci wafted from her smooth skin; the orange blossom and white flower scent left him yearning for more than just a kiss. He cupped the side of her face and ran a thumb over her cheek.

"Good luck, my beautiful witch," he said. "I'm just a button press away."

A flash of sorrow passed over her features. The emotion vanished so quickly Marcelo questioned if he really saw it. Instead of leaving, Sybil hesitated. Did she want to tell him something? He thought about how her mood had shifted on the way here. Should he probe and try to make her confess something?

Offering her a smile, Marcelo decided to let the matter rest. He again thought of her mysterious words from the blood studio, about him needing to understand. Sybil hadn't opened up to him that night, and it seemed she wouldn't do so now, either. If something bothered her, perhaps she would tell him on her own terms while he refrained from pushing the issue.

"I shall see you later," she said before pulling away and stepping out of the car.

Marcelo had planned on passing the time at the Bukowski Tavern, but his suddenly unquiet mind preferred seclusion while he waited for Sybil. He drove south on Blue Hill Avenue toward Harambee Park and sat in the near-empty bleachers of a baseball diamond to absently watch a late pick-up game under the lights.

As he swiped through local tourist sites and news bulletins on his phone, an article from Salem stunned him: *Unsolved Witch Attack.* Marcelo pressed the link. His eyes widened and mouth parted while he read.

Two women had been attacked in a home on Marlborough Road. One of them recovered, but the other lady, the homeowner, remained in a coma. The survivor claimed that an old woman had entered the residence and attacked for no apparent reason. Another witness, a neighbor doing yardwork, stated a young female had left the scene—dressed in the same outfit as the old woman.

"It can't be," Marcelo said as panic crept under his skin.

The metallic thump of a baseball bat striking a ball sounded from the field. Cheers, shouts, and curses erupted from the players as the batter rounded the bases. Marcelo rose and raced down the bleachers. He ran to his car and headed back the way he came.

"There has to be an explanation," he said to himself, weaving between lanes to get around slower traffic. "Sybil wouldn't do this. I know her."

Did he? Sybil came from a drastically different time period, one of chaos balanced on the edge of civilization and madness during colonization, wars, and religious fervor. She only woke from that anarchy a few days ago. He had imbibed her blood and shared her soul in a moment of passion, but that didn't mean he truly knew the deepest corners of the witch's mind.

If Sybil had committed the attack, perhaps she thought it would be easy to get away with. However, the young witch hadn't fully grasped how the modern world operated. She had much to learn about the instant transfer of information through police radio, news broadcasts, and other media. Sybil probably imagined people would be searching for an old woman, and that her restored youth sufficed to cover her tracks. She had also been in a hurry to leave Salem for Boston, another way to distance herself from the crime and keep Marcelo distracted.

He approached the residence and skidded into the driveway. Leaping out of the car, he ran up to the porch and smashed through the front door, hoping this was a huge mistake. Sybil and the homeowners would be sitting down for tea and cookies. His entrance would startle them, and she would chide him for making such a scene.

Instead of tea and cookies, broken furniture and two young children lay motionless on the carpet. Relief flooded Marcelo when he felt their strong pulses; the kids had only been stunned by some kind of spell. Down a hallway, a woman lay sprawled and bleeding from her forehead. Magic had not knocked her down. Instead, it seemed a blunt weapon had felled her.

A terrified shout sounded from upstairs. Water splashed, and someone struggled. Marcelo bounded up the steps and kicked open the bathroom door. The blackest of nightmares played out in front of him.

Despair smashed him in the chest as reality struck like a spear.

Sybil stood in front of a large bathtub, her hands motioning. A clothed man fought to escape from the tub. His arms and legs flailed as water doused the walls and floor. The man sat up and tried to pull himself out, but a tendril of water rose and wrapped around his neck. The liquid tightened and thrust him back under the surface.

Marcelo darted forward and grabbed Sybil's shoulder. She spun around and a disturbingly strong punch hammered his chin. He crashed into the wall and fell as chunks of plaster rained onto his head. She ran past him, and his foot lunged out. Sybil tripped and fell through the splintered doorway.

Marcelo climbed to his feet and tackled the witch when she tried to stand. They wrestled in the hallway and knocked pictures off the wall. Her entire body suddenly erupted in fire. Flames crackled over and around Marcelo. He shouted in pain and rolled away, his clothes and body smoking.

Sybil leapt up, and the fire on her vanished. Skin scorched, Marcelo rose gingerly and leaned on the banister as she raced down the stairs.

"Sybil!" he called. "Don't leave. Why are you doing this? Please, talk to me!"

She hesitated at the foot of the stairs, but did not turn around. "My pain hath burrowed too deep, Marcelo. I had a fair sight of my mother's death and could do nothing to prevent it. The inability to help her sickened me, I warrant. Thus, I fled England with my soul already torn. I also strove and failed to save Constance, then vowed that the descendants of those who murdered her shall perish. Truly, I hope in time you shall understand.

In all your years agone, have you ever loved someone so much that when you lost them to violence, it drove you mad?"

"No," Marcelo said softly. "But if you run out that door, then for me that experience will come to pass. I'm falling for you, Sybil, and I no longer feel alone with you at my side. But what you're doing is wrong. Don't let everything end like this."

She slowly turned to look up at him. Her eyes gleamed in longing, sparked in uncontrolled rage, then swam in uncertainty. Marcelo quickly leapt over the banister and landed on the first floor. Sybil stomped her foot, and a cloud of black smoke descended on him. He plowed through the dark haze and ran outside into the night, but she had disappeared.

Marcelo laid a hand over his chest. No heart beat or blood flowed, but that didn't mean his feelings remained dead and cold. A powerful sorrow swept over him. He turned to the porch and drove a fist through a wooden pillar, then squeezed his eyes shut when emotional pain ripped through him. Helplessness, confusion, and betrayal churned inside him. Anger threatened to explode into a complete loss of control, but grief and concern for Sybil quieted his rage.

"Help me," a weak voice called from indoors.

Marcelo burned to chase after Sybil, but these people needed his assistance. He would tend to their injuries and call an ambulance. Afterwards, he hoped to find Sybil before the police did.

Chapter Twelve

No Magic to Heal Heartache

Leaving the bedlam behind, Sybil ran away from the house in a random direction. Lost and out of breath, she eventually arrived at the Boston Public Library on Washington Street. She moved around the side of the building and slunk into the shadows to rest.

Her heart pounded and adrenaline dizzied her with nausea. Emotions surged and crushed her beneath relentless waves. Her mind soared in a hundred directions until she could no longer bear the turmoil. Mentally exhausted, Sybil lay down on the concrete and wept.

Marcelo…she had seen the utter desolation and disappointment on his face. She had shattered the trust between them and even hurt him physically with fire. Everything had worked out perfectly in Salem, and she had thought her actions in Boston would go smoothly as well. Marcelo now realized her deceit and true purpose of revenge.

I'm falling for you, Sybil, and I no longer feel alone with you at my side.

Even amidst the chaos in that house, his words and feelings had carried across the space between them.

His adoration burned inside her. She had wanted nothing more than to run back up those stairs and throw herself into his arms.

Trapped in this maddening world of endless racket and foreign culture, she had always felt safe with him. Their partnership had outgrown simply working together to stop Kendrick. Marcelo promised to help her, but it had been much more than that. He possessed a kind, generous nature, one that cared for society although most humans rejected him. He confessed to feeling alone and detached from civilization, the irony being a non-human like him worked hard to make life better for normal people. It represented his way of connecting to humanity, a way of dealing with the monster inside. He admitted Sybil had filled the emptiness in his life—and she promptly destroyed it by turning him down.

She also wished to be with Marcelo, but instead of saying the words, she had wounded him and run away. In that moment, her need for vengeance had trumped the most powerful sentiment of affection. Would he ever forgive her? Or, disagreeing with her methods, would he pursue her only to hand her over to the authorities?

Sybil rose from the ground and wiped her eyes on a sleeve. She took several deep, calming breaths and forced herself to regain her composure. Where should she go from here? Turning herself in to the police using a simple confession and apology would not make any of this disappear. Continuing to run wouldn't solve anything, either. Whatever option she chose, a peaceful, loving future at Marcelo's side now only existed in a dream.

With nothing else left, only pain and the ugly truth remained; she still desired vengeance against the rest of the descendants. At least one more lived in Boston, and she would have to hurry. Hopefully, Marcelo thought she would go into hiding.

Sybil used her limited phone skills to find transportation. She struggled to manipulate a taxi app, one of the features Marcelo had talked about before. Aggravated at how difficult it was for her to perform the simplest functions, she nearly threw the phone down. Yet eventually she summoned a carriage…a car, to come pick her up at the library.

She ignored the driver's attempt at conversation on the way to the second descendant's address in South Boston. Looking out the window at the night scene passing by, she wondered if she would ever truly comprehend these modern people and places. Without Marcelo, a heavy loneliness welled inside her. But she had to remain strong and focused on the task. Images of Constance swinging from the rope flashed in her mind. Too young and inexperienced to avenge her mother's murder, Sybil at least had a chance for retribution against Constance's executioners.

As for Kendrick, the mastermind behind all this, she would save his death for last. After hundreds of years of planning and waiting for her to awake, she felt confident the man lurked somewhere close by. Perhaps he waited in Salem where everything had begun. In any case, if she didn't locate him now, Kendrick was certain to find her sooner or later. She would then give him what he wanted—her new, powerful magic that would inflict massive suffering upon him before he died.

The taxi pulled up to the curb in front of her destination. Sybil paid the driver with some of the cash Marcelo had given her. She stepped out of the vehicle and observed the slatted dwelling, part of a chain of connected homes lining the narrow street. Those air-conditioning devices she had learned about protruded from windows.

Taking a deep breath, she observed the lighted glass panes set in the front door. She walked up four steps and rapped on the entrance. After a few tense moments, the door opened, and Marcelo appeared before her.

Sybil froze. How had he found her so quickly? Behind him, three frightened faces peered out at her. The magical ash marks stained two of the residents' hands, an older woman and a teenage boy.

"No more of this, Sybil," Marcelo said calmly. "Let's move away from here and talk."

She shook her head, a sour mixture of grief and fury bubbling inside her. "Then truly, you do not conceive my situation after all. This is my right, Marcelo. Through their blood line, these people shall pay for what happened to Constance, and for all the other victims who were tortured and hung years agone. Depart forthwith and be gone from my sight!"

A dangerous light shone in Marcelo's eyes, a hard gaze she had never seen before. His voice may have sounded casual, but his rigid posture indicated he had expected a confrontation. She realized he would protect these citizens at all cost.

"Leave this house," he said in the quiet tone that served as both a plea and a threat.

Sybil glanced at the family huddled behind him. Although separated from the Salem Witch Trials by over three hundred years, she did not see an innocent couple and their frightened son. She instead saw the frenzied rock-throwers, the magistrates, the thugs, and the hangman out for witch blood. To these people, the trials were ancient history on display in a museum. Sybil's nightmares, terror, and sacrifice in that era had turned into selfies and souvenirs for ignorant modern citizens. To her, the trauma happened only days ago before waking from her slumber. The agony, sorrow, and torment still lingered inside—as did her insatiable need for justice.

Sybil thrust her hands forward, and a blast of air slammed into Marcelo's chest. The force knocked him into a shelf filled with books and DVDs. Screaming, the family scrambled away and Sybil charged into the home.

Wind rushed, and a blur of color raced by her. Using preternatural speed, Marcelo traveled across the living room and materialized in front of Sybil. He shoved her backward, and she fell onto a small table supporting a lamp. The bulbs shattered, and the shade crushed under her body as the table collapsed.

Rising from the debris, she sent a torrent of picture frames sailing toward him. The photos tore from walls and lifted from shelves to pelt his body. Growling, he charged through the attack as frames and glass smashed against his face and chest. His hand wrapped around her throat. He lifted Sybil by the neck and tossed her through the living room window.

Crashing through the glass, she summoned a roaring gust of wind to cushion her fall. The airstream wrapped her body like a blanket as she hit the asphalt outside. The spell saved her from a bone-jarring impact, but the tumble still left her dazed and breathless.

Marcelo sprinted out the front door and met Sybil on the street. His shoes crunched over broken glass. The neighborhood block had come alive; lights snapped on and residents peeked from windows and doorways. In the distance, the wail of a police siren grew louder as it neared.

"You cannot prevent my destiny," Sybil said, standing. "I shall see this through, I warrant!"

Marcelo's face softened. Yearning filled his eyes, and hope glinted in an anxious gaze. "This is not your destiny," he replied. "You are capable of greater and more wonderful things. I want to help you find your place in this new world, Sybil. Please stop this madness. You've already hurt people, and despite what you may feel, this is not the way. I will never leave you even if we fight for eternity. Just come home with me, I beg you."

Sybil's heart cried for her to surrender. All she had to do was go to him and be at peace. However, nothing in her life had ever been easy. She had only known anguish, tragedy, and loss. Unable to escape those terrible experiences, they had molded her into a relentless and callous monster that burned to correct the injustices, even if it meant leaving Marcelo.

"I am sorry," she whispered.

Sybil spread her arms as tears blurred her vision. Tiny bolts of lightning danced on her palms, then raced up her arms and spread down her body and legs until she glowed in crackling light. Loud thunder boomed in the street. The lightning covering her brightened until Marcelo threw an arm over his eyes.

Sybil's surroundings changed in a flash. She appeared on another street containing different homes. Her experimental teleportation spell had worked, but she had no idea where she now stood. Controlling her destination and accuracy would eventually come.

Teleporting also had a limited range; she more than likely only moved a couple blocks from her previous location.

Either way, Marcelo would not be able to follow her easily. She needed to find a safe haven and perform another location spell, this time with a map of the United States to reveal even more descendants. However, her supply of magic items had run out. She might be able to restock in Boston, but this city seemed so large and dynamic. She didn't recognize anything here, not like in Salem where she felt more at home in witch territory. She also needed to distance herself from Marcelo. Sybil doubted she could avoid him for long, but she could at least get a head start.

After a few concentrated moments of taps and swipes on her scratched-up phone, she discovered the MBTA Commuter Rail Line, which ran between Boston's North Station and Salem. She summoned another taxi, and the driver left her at the train station where she headed inside to purchase a ticket for Salem.

Chapter Thirteen

Demon Unleashed

After his violent encounter with Sybil in South Boston, Marcelo walked toward his car parked down the road. A whirlwind of emotions mauled him. Denial warped his sense of reality. How did it all come to this? Everything had happened so fast. His contentment and newfound adoration for Sybil had been turned upside down. Mesmerized by her history, charm, and beauty, his feelings ushered in thoughts of a relationship after the business with Kendrick finished. He had settled into a state of bliss and failed to detect the warning signs.

Now it was too late. In Salem, Sybil had put a woman in a coma and nearly killed a man here in Boston. Undeterred by her fight against Marcelo, she then traveled to her next target to continue her path of destruction. And once again, she had ignored his interference and disappeared without a word.

Marcelo's hands knotted into fists. Anger and desperation clenched his jaw. His heels struck the pavement in long, irritated strides. Dark feelings smothered his senses, and he failed to notice the three human males waiting in the shadows as he approached the rented BMW.

"Yo, vampire!" a voice called.

Wearing a Red Sox jersey and jeans, a man carrying a baseball bat emerged from an alley. The strong scent of gasoline wafted from the soaked towel wrapped around the end of the bat. Two other men, one wielding a chain and the other a knife, stepped out as well.

"We saw what happened down the street, fang boy," the first man said. "You wreck our neighborhood, and you're just going to walk away? I know the vamps around Boston, and you're not one of them. So we're here to send you off and make sure you never return."

Marcelo paid the man no attention. His thoughts resided with Sybil and what he should do next. Provided she didn't figure out their phones were linked, he could track her down at any time using the GPS function. But he realized that finding her only meant rescuing one of her victims, not winning her heart back. Sybil had made it clear she wanted nothing to do with him.

An unbearable emotional pain erupted inside Marcelo. When he again confronted the woman he desired, they would face each other as enemies.

Something cold and sharp penetrated his side. Snapping out of his reverie, he glanced down and saw a knife wedged underneath his ribs. He gazed into the narrowed eyes of the man who had just stabbed him.

"Welcome to South Boston, you undead freak," the attacker said in a sneer.

A flaming baseball bat crashed into the side of Marcelo's head. His hair caught on fire, and his skin sizzled. The smell of burnt, undead flesh filled his nostrils. A chain wrapped around his legs and jerked him off his feet. Marcelo struck the asphalt and cried out in pain and frustration. Distracted by his sour mood over

Sybil, he had been careless and vulnerable to the well-coordinated assault.

Smoke and flames wrapped half of his head, and he could hardly see or concentrate. The blurred form of one of the men threw something. Gasoline splashed on Marcelo's upper body as he struggled on the street. The blazing bat flew down toward his head. He blocked it with a forearm, but the dancing flames caught on his doused clothing and the fire spread to his chest.

An uncontrollable rage exploded within him. Tearing the chain from his legs, he leapt up and slammed a fist into the knife-wielder's jaw, knocking him unconscious. The thug wearing the Red Sox shirt swung the baseball bat again. Marcelo ducked the blow and grabbed the assailant, then threw him toward a lamp post. The man crashed into the metal pole and fell, unmoving.

The last ruffian who had thrown the chain and gasoline turned and fled. On fire, Marcelo snarled and leapt into the air. He left a trail of smoke and landed in front of the fleeing attacker. Digging his fingers into his opponent's shoulders, Marcelo leaned forward and sank his fangs into the man's neck.

Warm, fresh blood poured into his mouth. The demon soul thirsted, its feral nature howling in contentment. The man's heart thundered in terror and anguish. Marcelo tasted adrenaline and fear in the blood, an intoxicating mixture that spurred his hunger even more. His hands tightened, and the man's body fell limp, the heart slowing towards death.

This is what you are! the demon inside Marcelo screamed. *Blood studios and straws...how weak and pathetic you have become.*

A nearby scream erupted in the night. The terrified shriek—a very *human* sound of distress and reality—broke the feeding frenzy. He released the victim and the thug dropped onto the sidewalk, scarcely breathing. Marcelo tore the shirt off the man's body and used it to snuff out the flames on his own head and chest.

"Steve, hurry call nine-one-one!" a woman in a window shouted. "A vampire just killed three people outside!"

Marcelo hadn't killed anyone; the men would live. However, that didn't excuse the brutal and senseless act he had just committed. He hadn't lost control like this in decades. Not once in the last fifty years had he bitten a human out of spite and the desire to not only inflict harm…but to *kill*.

Shock rooted him to the street. "What have I done?" he asked the darkness.

Marcelo should have attempted to escape the situation. Although the fire pained him, his body would heal and sustain no permanent damage. Using his superior strength and speed, he could have fled the scene or pushed the men to the ground without causing real harm.

Instead, he had allowed the demon soul lurking inside have its way. Emotionally unstable, Marcelo had needed a way to unleash his stress and anger, and the situation on the street presented itself at the wrong time. But he couldn't blame the demon soul—Marcelo *was* the demon. A dark part of him wanted to hurt those men and taste blood, a part that would always exist no matter how cultured and modernized he became.

During the old days in the Americas before the Europeans arrived, he had done his share of killing for blood. His hunting grounds had stretched across South America, Central, and North America. Over the centuries, times changed and civilization advanced. Society allowed undead the option of ingesting blood in safe and harmless ways.

Just like anyone else—human or otherwise—Marcelo existed as a being with moral choices to make in life. He had made a terrible one tonight that would haunt him for the rest of his days. He could no longer judge Sybil. Marcelo had become a hypocrite by almost killing that man; the woman's scream barely stopped him. Just like the young witch, he had regressed into a lost fugitive trying to find a place in the world.

Intense, powerful shame lowered his gaze to the pavement. Humbled by his repulsive actions and weak will, Marcelo had nothing left but to chase Sybil and at least protect more innocent people. Far from a hero, he was only another monster on the street trying to hide his fangs in civilization's shadow.

The blare of police sirens urged him to sprint to his car. He dove behind the wheel, and the engine roared as he sped away. Marcelo winced while his flesh healed for the second time that night. The singed hair grew out and the blackened, peeled skin regained its original smooth texture by the time he reached the Eliot Hotel.

In the room, he packed his and Sybil's things. After checking out, Marcelo cruised onto Interstate 90 and rode north toward Boston Logan International Airport. He pulled over at Bremen Street Park to check his phone and saw that Sybil had made it to Boston North Station. After waiting twenty more minutes, the GPS signal indicated she had boarded a train headed for Salem.

Marcelo returned to the interstate and continued north until he merged onto the Salem Turnpike. Reaching Salem, he checked back into the Hawthorne Hotel and asked for the same room he had before, which thankfully remained unoccupied. He entered and absently unpacked the suitcases, then later realized he had neatly arranged Sybil's things as if she would return at any moment.

He gazed at the sofa where they had spent hours talking about the modern world. Whether he conversed with the old Sybil or the young, her curious, intelligent, witty, and courageous demeanor had captivated him. Her spirited eyes and brilliant smile bathed him like the cheery sun used to centuries ago. Her vigorous interest in everything from bubblegum to Clint Eastwood movies motivated him to tell her anything she wanted to know.

Pouring some wine, he sat and watched the GPS indicate her arrival at the Coach House Inn, a bed and breakfast located on Lafayette Street north of Salem State University. There the signal remained, where exhaustion after an endless night more than likely had her crashing out as soon as she checked in.

Marcelo missed Sybil Radella Cotterill and yearned for her with his undying heart. Its beat had ended a long time ago, but his affection would endure forever…if only she would have him again.

Chapter Fourteen

The Wyman Woods Coven

Moving through the darkened trees, Kendrick's flashlight illuminated the underbrush of the Wyman Woods, a thirty-three-acre forest in Marblehead just outside of Salem. He cursed at the thick growth, the insects, and the long walk. Worst of all, the witches still hadn't given him a wood sprite, the final ingredient for his spell to control Marcelo. If the Wyman Woods coven had reneged on their promise, he would slaughter them on this very night.

He strolled beneath the shadowed leaf canopy and eventually crossed into a small meadow amid the trees. He turned off the flashlight and observed a group of five witches in the middle of a ritual. Torches on long staffs blazed around the circle of three robed women and two men. The group danced and moved around a wooden altar, chanting and beating on tambourines. Candles burned on the surface, and an old tome lay open next to a miniature cauldron.

Kendrick gazed into the starry sky over the meadow and enjoyed the mystical energy tingling over his skin. The coven had summoned this energy through their dance and music in preparation for magical work. The spiritual power source vibrated the earth beneath their feet. The air hummed with vigor. Soon the group stopped and knelt in a ring around the altar, each witch representing an elemental point on the pentagram.

"Beautiful, isn't it?" a female voice suddenly asked at his side.

Kendrick nearly jumped out of his skin. Very few beings on the planet could approach him without his sensing it first. Cessani, the leader of the Wyman Woods coven, was one of them.

"Yes, it is," he answered. "But it's a shame I'll have to destroy the ritual, and your witches, unless you've brought me what I require."

Cessani smiled. Starlight played in her robust eyes, yet a timeworn face reflected her old age. Silver streaks ran through her loose black hair. A red robe draped her thin, slightly bent frame, her bare feet tucked into the grass. "No need to get upset, Umaq. I have what you need right here." She held out a cloth covered jar.

"I really wish you wouldn't call me that," said Kendrick.

He took the jar and unwrapped the cloth. A light shone from inside the glass, the source a tiny wood sprite sitting with her knees drawn to her chest. Instead of hair, crooked twigs sprouted from her head. For clothes, grass clippings covered her frame. Her translucent wings drooped, the gesture matching her downcast expression. The sprite must have realized her fate—a sacrifice for his spell.

Kendrick rewrapped the jar and tucked it under an arm. "Good. I would hate to lose you as an ally, Cessani. I am too close to transforming this world and achieving victory. Great power, and anything else you want, will be yours as long as you cooperate."

"You don't need to remind me, Umaq," she said using extra emphasis on the name. "Hundreds of years may separate our births, but we are both motivated by similar interests. You are a layqa, a very powerful spellcrafter from the days of the Inca, and I am a modern witch. I appreciate and desire the ancient days when our kind ruled without fear or competition. I want true reverence in the eyes of the public, not Halloween costumes and hobbyists playing with magic. It is time for the legitimacy of witchcraft to reclaim itself in the world."

"I like your enthusiasm, but I wouldn't rely on the gods to help you," Kendrick replied. He nodded toward the ritual. "Your coven is interacting with the Triple Moon Goddess—the Maiden, Mother, and Crone. I already told you about the meddling of Inti, the sun god, and the incompetence of other old gods. You need to stay away from the deities and trust in yourself, Cessani. The true power lies within you."

"You shouldn't speak such blasphemy." She gazed up at the sky. "Do you see the sliver of the waxing moon? The Maiden is watching tonight. One of the principal things she represents is new beginnings, which is what you and I want. The Wyman Woods coven will worship and respect her. Whether people call her Persephone, Brigid, Nimue, or other historical names, the Maiden has my adoration, and she will provide."

Kendrick scoffed. "Do as you wish. Just be prepared, as my familiar, Sebas, reported that Sybil and Marcelo are back in Salem. I had originally planned to bewitch Marcelo while a growing relationship brought him and Sybil together. However, I didn't anticipate them having such a nasty fight. But their conflict may work out for the better. Marcelo's emotions are stretched thin, and his mind is a mess. He'll be more susceptible to spell manipulation in that state."

"I don't doubt you'll be successful," said Cessani. "We'll be ready to support you when the time comes. Now if you'll excuse me, I must complete the ritual with my coven."

Kendrick shifted the jar to his other arm. "The Inca moon goddess, Mama Quilla, would be jealous of you worshiping the young Maiden. Hardly anyone acknowledges Quilla anymore. As she is one of the old gods that never did anything for me, that makes me smile."

Walking into the meadow, Cessani stopped to glance back at him. "What makes you think I don't speak to Mama Quilla as well? She's rather attentive if you just give her the time."

With a knowing smile that made Kendrick shiver, Cessani entered the circle of torches and knelt before the altar.

Chapter Fifteen

New Alliances

In the Coach House Inn, Sybil woke late in the day, still tired and sore from battling Marcelo. She took a long bath and tried not to think about how little cash she had left. She couldn't afford another night in any hotel. The last of the funds would be spent today on magical ingredients for an additional location spell.

After eating the continental breakfast in her room, Sybil hit the streets to buy the required materials. She used the map function on her phone to locate several witchcraft stores north of her hotel. She walked about a mile on Lafayette before reaching the district that housed the Hawthorne Hotel and Salem Witch Museum.

Several witch supply shops clustered the area on various roads. White Light Pentacles, Enchanted, and Artemisia Botanicals were some of the places she visited. It took several stops before she felt satisfied with the quality of her ingredients. Since she would be using a map of the entire United States, she needed the spell to be more powerful and accurate than before.

With her items stuffed in bags, Sybil sat on a bench to rest her aching feet. More shopping remained as she still needed a yard of natural cordage for knot magic. A good cord consisted of the fibrous cambium layer between the wood and the outer bark of a tree. So far, she hadn't been able to find any. One additional store sat nearby, but she had eluded the Crow Haven Corner to avoid thinking of Marcelo.

This was the shop he had taken her to across from the Hawthorne, the day he had braved the sun in his silly outfit in order to help her. She remembered how excited he had been. His enthusiasm had made her feel more confident in her abilities.

Dark, pungent guilt chewed her insides. Despite all he had done for her, she lied to him that entire day. Marcelo thought she searched for family, but all the while she only used him to advance her mission of revenge. She destroyed the trust between them and had witnessed his devastating pain in Boston when he first discovered her ploy. She would never forget his stunned, wounded gaze, staring at her as if she had transformed into a hideous monster.

In many ways, she had.

A hollow pit had formed in her soul, and a black flame burned in its depths. Her light had been stuffed in that hole, suffocating, slowly extinguished by the damage she inflicted on people…and on herself. Marcelo had a way of filling the emptiness and bringing forth her illumination. His patience, kindness, and support had opened the way for Sybil to shine, but she had elected to dig the pit even deeper.

She longed for his touch, the way his cool skin warmed against her body. Sharing her blood with him, she had opened her mind and broken soul to a range of intimacy and connection she never experienced before.

Despite the blackness inside her, the beginnings of love for Marcelo had bloomed in the hollow pit. But as her path took her farther away from him, Sybil could only reflect on the past and lament on what could have been.

The afternoon wore on and she still had much work to do. Sybil rose from the bench and walked toward the Crow Haven Corner. She entered the shop and browsed for her cord, then panicked when she checked her pocket and realized not enough money remained for her to eat afterwards. Stomach grumbling, she tried to think of a solution that didn't require robbery or harming people.

Sybil located the natural cord of tree fiber and paid for it at the register. She hefted her bags from the other stores, then paused when spotting a familiar, middle-aged woman chatting near the entrance. Her blond hair sat packed into a large bun on the back of her head. A memory of this person came to mind, the amateur witch who had offered to help with her magic. She also spoke about starting a new coven, then presented a business card. In response, Sybil had acted rude and insulted the lady.

Not wanting another awkward encounter, Sybil turned to leave, then realized she had been in her elderly state during the initial meeting. The woman would not be able to recognize her now.

A desperate plan formed in her mind. Hungry and without money, maybe she could befriend the woman and receive another invitation. Food was certain to follow, and if the situation continued in a positive manner, perhaps a temporary place to stay as well.

Sybil approached the lady and smiled. "Good day. I beg your pardon for the interruption. A friend of mine, a vampire you met hither some days agone, spoke of you. He gave forth your description and made me conversant about your new coven."

The woman's face brightened, and delight filled her blue eyes. Color bloomed on her cheeks as she spoke. "Oh, yes! I remember Marcelo who was all bundled up for a day in the sun. His older companion acted impolite, but he was the perfect gentleman." She extended a hand. "I'm Grace. I love how you speak, by the way. It's too cute and fits perfectly in Salem. Have you been practicing that form of speech for long?"

Grace…that was it. Sybil couldn't recall her name. "My name is Sybil," she said, shaking the hand. "I…I have practiced the speech for many months agone. Of a truth, I have also practiced witchcraft. It would please me to learn more about your coven, if you have time this afternoon."

"Of course I have time!" Grace expressed in an excited tone. "I wasn't planning on visitors today, but I'd love it if you came over." She handed Sybil a card, the same one she had passed to Marcelo the first time. "Be at my place in an hour."

Sybil pocketed the card. "Thank you, Grace. I shall meet you at yonder cottage." She started walking away, but the woman called out.

"Oh, how is Marcelo, by the way? He's invited as well, if you can drag him out of his coffin." Grace laughed as if she had told the best joke in the world.

Sybil forced a grin. "I shall give him a call, though he hath other business, I warrant. Fare well." She turned and hurried out of the store.

Outside, Sybil used her phone to locate the address listed on Grace's card. Not having a charger, she grew uneasy at the red battery indication that threatened to power down her device. Grace lived about three miles away, south of Salem State University near Highway 1A. With no money for a taxi, she started walking carrying her purchases. She hoped a normal pace would allow her to arrive around the specified time of one hour.

Sweaty and fatigued from the warm afternoon stroll, Sybil reached Grace's white, two-story house on Cleveland Road. Large potted plants stood guard in front of the raised wooden porch. A red car sat parked on a small strip of asphalt next to the home. Perched above two second floor windows, a third attic window overlooked the quiet street.

Sybil rapped on the door, and a beaming Grace welcomed her inside. "Sybil, you look exhausted! And are those the same bags you had at the Crow Haven Corner?" She glanced outside. "Wait…don't tell me you walked here. Goodness, child, why didn't you tell me? I could have given you a ride."

"It is not a problem, I warrant," Sybil replied, setting her things down. Three cats, one gray, one black, and the other orange and white, appeared from nowhere and began sniffing her bags and feet. "I am just troubled that I could not bring you forth a gift."

"Never mind, sweet thing," Grace responded.

She ushered Sybil to a table in the kitchen, then handed her a large glass of iced tea and a plate of cheese and crackers. "The chicken in the oven should be done shortly. I love making food for guests, so I hope you're hungry. I'll give you the skinny on my coven. But I'm mostly glad to meet new people, even if they don't join. I'm so pleased you came, Sybil."

"Truly, I am grateful to you for hosting me, Grace, and feel happy I came hither. I dwell in…in Boston and am visiting Salem for a few days. I shall attend Salem State next semester. To aid with tuition, I hoped to find work and a place to dwell nearby. My heart is excited to begin college, but more nervous than anything, I warrant."

Sybil had invented this story during her walk, a way to speak with Grace and cover her true purpose of needing food and lodging. Even if only for a day, she hated lying to the good-hearted woman. Fabricating tales was all Sybil did lately, and it reminded her of deceiving Marcelo.

"College!" Grace exclaimed. "Oh sweetie, you don't look a day out of high school and you're already planning your future." She moved about the kitchen to prepare the meal. "That's wonderful, and I wish you luck. I'm sure you'll do just fine."

The older witch sat down and poured some tea, then told Sybil a little about herself. She had married young, divorced after two years, and had a twenty-year-old son living in Worcester. She lived by herself in Salem and worked as a secretary in Marblehead.

Grace served the full meal of baked chicken, mashed potatoes, corn, and buttered biscuits. Not knowing when her next meal would arrive, Sybil wolfed her food. She also wondered where she would sleep tonight. Asking this woman so soon to provide a room seemed awkward and unrealistic.

Ice cream followed the chicken, then coffee and a lengthy, detailed account of Grace's fledgling coven. Sybil listened with interest, her prior hate and ridicule of novices and modern magic gone. Passion moved Grace as she explained. Her animated gestures and excitement made Sybil appreciate the woman even more. Displaying humble pride and motivation, Grace acted very serious and professional about witchcraft and her coven. If Sybil's life hadn't been shredded by turmoil, she would have enjoyed being a member of the woman's group.

Hours passed and night painted the kitchen window black. A loud knock on the door halted their conversation.

"I'm not expecting anyone else," Grace said, rising from the table and heading for the living room. "Who could it be?"

Sybil's heart raced. Her body warred between freezing on the spot and dashing out the back door. Tension knotted her fists. Had Marcelo found her? Did the night watch—the police—discover her identity as the culprit in the multi-city crimes? Butterflies rioted in her belly. Sweat moistened her lower back. Fighting and running had exhausted her. With emotions shattered, she almost felt like giving up.

Grace opened the front door, and Sybil heard her gasp in surprise. "Cessani! What are you doing here?"

"Good evening, Grace," a woman's voice said from the doorway. "I apologize for the intrusion, but I must speak with the girl, Sybil."

"How do you know her, and more importantly, how did you realize she was here?" Grace asked, her tone wary. "Have you been spying on my house? I already told you I'm not interested in joining your coven. I have my own, thank you very much."

"I'm not here to talk about the coven. Please, I must see Sybil. Her life is in danger tonight."

Sybil left the kitchen and moved to the front door. An elderly woman with silver-streaked black hair stood on the porch. She wore a simple, long-patterned dress and an open knit sweater.

Grace slipped an arm around Sybil's waist in a protective gesture. "The young lady is my guest, Cessani. Please don't involve Sybil in whatever odd differences you and I may have. Whatever you believe is happening, I'm sure she's perfectly safe with me."

Cessani ignored Grace as she looked at Sybil. "I've heard so much about you, Sybil. Please hear what I have to say. This matter concerns a very dangerous man you are acquainted with—Kendrick. He's right here in Salem."

"Kendrick!" Sybil called out. Agitated, her suspicion increased by the second as she glared at the woman. "How are you conversant with him, and of me?"

Cessani sighed and shifted her feet. "Grace, can I please come in and sit? I'm too old to tell stories while standing on a porch."

Grace hesitated, then looked at Sybil wearing motherly concern. "Only if you give permission, dear."

"I do. I must hear Cessani speak forthwith."

Grace moved aside and motioned for the older woman to enter. The three of them sat in the living room.

"All right," Cessani began as she settled on the couch. "First of all, Sybil, Kendrick's real name is Umaq. He's an ancient Inca and a layqa, a witch, but that's a story for another time.

"Years ago, I met him at a silly Halloween party one of my friends dragged me to. Anyway, I wouldn't say Umaq and I became friends, but more like respected associates. He impressed me with his lore of witchcraft and offered to teach my coven new and powerful ways to perform magic. I learned a lot from him—unique, fantastic, and somewhat frightening methods of spell-work. I grew obsessed with learning styles of witchcraft I never dreamed of. We operated well together, and a bond formed between us.

"Umaq eventually told me your story, Sybil. I didn't believe him until I snuck into the Salem Witch Museum and saw you inside that storeroom coffin. Over three hundred years you've slept and have grown very powerful. His plan is to bewitch your friend, Marcelo, and use him to turn you into a vampire. Somehow, Umaq will then be able to control you. You are to lead his army of demons after he unleashes them upon the world by using portals at Machu Picchu in Peru. He then wants to slay the Inca sun god, Inti. Afterwards, he will proclaim himself ruler during a reign of darkness."

The color drained from Grace's face. She fanned her cheeks and appeared ready to faint.

Rage boiled inside Sybil. All fear dissipated in a cloud of steam. The threat to her life didn't bother her, but hearing that danger also shadowed Marcelo pushed her over the edge. She trembled on the sofa. Kendrick, or Umaq, had turned out to be much more than a mysterious, wicked minister in old Salem Village. If everything Cessani claimed proved true, it didn't surprise Sybil that the yellow-eyed man had worked with demons to achieve his sick goal of conquest.

"Tell me where Umaq dwells forthwith," Sybil demanded. "I shall kill him tonight."

"Child, I didn't warn you so you could storm off and confront him," said Cessani. "Umaq is more powerful than you know. Even with your super-charged abilities, you're no match for him. He's been planning this for centuries. It will take much more than a head-on attack to stop that maniac."

Restless, Sybil stood and paced the living room while running fingers through her hair. "Wherefore did you tell me then? Shall you stop him? Centuries agone, Umaq encouraged the witch hysteria in Salem Village. I had a fair sight of my beloved friend as she died, Cessani. Truly, you should have suspected something evil after working with him hitherto. As a witch, I refuseth to believe you would aid a monster like him."

"I'm not helping him," Cessani stated. "That's why I'm confessing everything. I realized too late his ultimate goal would only bring destruction and chaos. I came to protect you, Sybil. My coven is more than capable of doing so. Umaq believes I support him, which is why I'm still alive. To maintain his trust, I've done some terrible things I'm not proud of. I may never be able to atone, but at least I can try to thwart his plans."

"I do not desire protection," Sybil replied. "If I travel forth with you, then it shall be to destroy Umaq."

Cessani looked down into her lap. Distress dominated her wrinkled features, then fear as dark brown eyes glanced up at Sybil. "We would be fools, but perhaps together we can achieve victory." Grunting softly, she stood from the sofa. "Come, Sybil. While we form a plan, you can find sanctuary in the Wyman Woods with my coven. Umaq and his demons will hunt you, but I promise you'll be safe among the trees."

Shaking off her initial shock, Grace finally stood and placed a hand on Sybil's shoulder. "My head is spinning from all this! I am out of the loop and have a hundred questions, but something doesn't seem right,

Sybil. Since Cessani and I have had our spats in the past, this may sound personal, but I don't trust her." The motherly concern from before returned to her kind gaze. "Stay with me," Grace continued. "I'm not the most adept witch, but I'll protect you with all my heart and soul."

Sybil blushed, but not due to warm feelings of friendship from her new companion. Instead, deep remorse heated her cheeks, the same guilt she experienced when lying to Marcelo about her family. She had already deceived Grace just to get a meal. Now the woman had offered to sacrifice her wellbeing for Sybil. Grace's life would not be put at risk. Not for someone like Sybil, who had only harmed people since rising from her centuries-old slumber.

"Thank you, Grace, but I must depart," Sybil replied, her heart aching. The hurt look from Grace troubled her even more. "Cessani is correct. Of a truth, Umaq is extremely dangerous and I do not wish you any harm." She nodded to Cessani, then walked to the front door. "We shall go."

Misery wrapped Sybil as she stepped outside with Cessani. She refrained from saying goodbye to Grace for fear of bursting into tears. Her rude departure had been on purpose, an act to ensure her new friend stayed far away from the volatile situation.

Riding in Cessani's car, Sybil pulled out her phone to call Marcelo. Her thumb hovered over his name…then backed out of the call list. Warning him about Umaq would only drag Marcelo closer to the situation. If the malicious plan involved him turning her into a vampire, then keeping Marcelo far away remained the best course of action.

As if fate agreed, the battery indication on the phone beeped a final time and the device powered down. She could have asked if Cessani had a charger or phone to borrow, but Sybil decided to let the matter rest. Her only hope was that Marcelo would give up on everything and return back home to California. She couldn't stand the thought of Umaq trying to harm him. But if things worked out with Cessani and the Wyman Woods coven, then Umaq would soon be dead.

Chapter Sixteen

Yellow Eyes, Black Heart

Not feeling very talkative, Sybil rode in silence on the way to Cessani's house in Marblehead. Perhaps lost in her own thoughts, the older witch didn't offer much conversation as she drove east from south Salem. The night had grown late. Stars shone bright and whispered of warm beds and sleep. Cessani eventually pulled into a small cluster of homes on Rainbow Road, just south of the main bulk of the Wyman Woods.

After parking in the driveway, Sybil yawned and got out of the car. Several trees and bushes dotted the large front yard. A heavy silence smothered the area, and an awful smell hovered. She wrinkled her nose and stepped around the vehicle, then halted when she saw that something troubled Cessani.

The old woman stood tense. Her concerned gaze swept the sky. She then glanced around the yard, her hands knotted in fists. Fear widened her eyes when she looked at Sybil.

"Walk with me," Cessani whispered. "Do not speak or make a sound."

Heart thumping in trepidation, Sybil joined the elder witch and together they moved toward the porch.

Stopping suddenly, Cessani grabbed Sybil's upper arm and pointed.

The door stood halfway open. Grooves had slashed into the wood as if by a huge claw. The bad odor from before intensified, emanating from inside the dwelling. A low growl rumbled from the shadows. Something moved within the house. Half covered in darkness, a skinless shoulder, arm, and leg appeared in the entryway. A splash sounded on the wooden floor, and a dozen gray worms slithered outside.

"We need to leave!" Cessani cried. "Umaq knows I've betrayed him. We must flee to the woods for protection!"

The old woman took Sybil's hand and hauled her through the grass around the side of the home. Any notion of fighting vanished from Sybil's mind. After seeing that thing in the doorway, she wanted to escape as far as possible. A grotesque terror lurked in that house, something she had never seen before. Fear pumped her legs and kept her from looking back.

Reaching the backyard fence, Cessani threw the latch on a small gate and continued through, hauling Sybil.

"The Wyman Woods are like my second home," Cessani uttered in gasps as they ran. "That creature has no power there."

"What was yonder thing?" Sybil asked, still not daring to look back.

They entered the darkness beneath the trees, but Cessani's pace didn't falter. She moved through the undergrowth, over protruding roots, and between trunks in ease. The old woman really did know the woods. Sybil had no trouble keeping up with Cessani's firm, guiding grip on her hand.

"That was one of Umaq's strongest demons, Nala'thelx," the witch replied. "We're almost there."

A long, terrifying howl rocked the forest. Goosebumps erupted over Sybil's skin, and her heart banged inside her chest. The unearthly wail shook the trees. Branches swayed, and leaves rattled…or had it just been a breeze?

Either way, Sybil kept running. Soon flickers of light appeared between some trees ahead. She entered a clearing, and the bright stars welcomed her after the stifling darkness beneath the thick canopy. A ring of head-high torches burned in the meadow. Within the circle, a large wooden post thrust from the ground.

"Come inside the ring of fire, for it is sacred earth," said Cessani.

Sybil entered, and a sudden feeling of weight dropped on her shoulders. Her legs buckled under the strain, and she cried out. Intense pressure squeezed her onto the grass. She could barely raise her head to glare at Cessani.

"Wha…what is th-this?" Sybil asked through gritted teeth. Her muscles trembled in effort. Shaking, she managed to push herself up to her hands and knees.

"A precaution," Cessani answered as she stepped into the circle of flaming torches. The crushing phenomenon did not affect the old witch. She stood over Sybil and smiled. "You're much too powerful to take chances with. A handy spell to weaken you was necessary."

Bushes rustled all around the clearing. Three robed women and two men stepped out of the trees and stood evenly around the ring.

"Meet my coven," Cessani continued. "They are going to tie you up so you'll be presentable for Umaq."

"You double-crossing hag!" Sybil shouted. The effort winded her, and she gasped for air. She lifted an arm to cast a spell, but the mystical pressure slammed her hand back down and pressed it against the grass.

"Resisting will only cause you more pain," said Cessani. She nodded to the others, and the coven entered the circle.

The group lifted Sybil and pushed her against the large pole in the center. Rough hands tied her arms behind the post and bound her feet together. Cessani grabbed Sybil's chin and forced her mouth open. The old witch brought a flask to Sybil's lips and poured a sour liquid into her mouth. She spit the fluid into Cessani's face.

One of the men slammed his fist into Sybil's stomach. Pain ruptured in her belly, and she groaned. Already exhausted by the heavy mystical force, she couldn't even struggle as her body sagged in the bindings. Cessani gripped Sybil's chin once more. Weakened, she failed to resist as the liquid flowed into her mouth. The man pinched her nostrils and forced her mouth shut. Sybil had no choice but to swallow.

The sour fluid went down her throat. What felt like glass fragments exploded in her stomach. The sharp, grinding sensation spread to her limbs until her entire body suffered from stabbing needles. Sybil whimpered in agony. Hot tears slid down her cheeks.

The torment eventually stopped as did the magical pressure weighing her down. Sweaty and gasping, Sybil opened her eyes and glanced around the small meadow. The coven had knelt around the circle, each person next to a torch. Cessani stood off to the side and looked back toward the tree line.

A shadow stepped out of the woods and headed for the circle. The figure swished through the grass and into the firelight. Recognition struck Sybil like a hammer—those sickly yellow eyes and the brown, wrinkled face of tree bark. Minister Kendrick, the cruel man called Umaq, approached her and bowed.

"Sybil Radella Cotterill, it has been quite some years," he said. "Centuries, more accurately. I hope you are well rested after your slumber."

She tried to conjure a spell to incinerate his face, but Cessani's foul drink had done something to her. She could barely concentrate, let alone summon the strength and energy to utilize magic. Long ago, Umaq had witnessed Sybil escape the noose with her power. It seemed he had gone through extensive preparations to prevent such a getaway this time.

"I shall kill you," she said, breathing heavily. "Nothing can stop me, I warrant."

"Now there's an accent and diction I haven't spoken in ages," Umaq observed. "But boldly stated, Miss Cotterill. Your courage has not faltered since the Colonies. It's a shame your friend Constance didn't share in your bravado. Perhaps she could have saved herself in that tree."

Sybil strained with all her might. The ropes pinning her rustled, and the wooden post creaked. A sharp wind whipped through the area and nearly extinguished the torches. The coven glanced around and murmured in alarm, but Cessani put up a silencing hand.

"Stand fast," the old witch called out. "Sybil is just putting on a show. She can't harm any of us."

"Oh, but she will certainly try," said Umaq, bringing his face closer to Sybil's. "It takes my strongest magic and Cessani's best abilities to keep you in check, yet you still fight. What a fantastic specimen you are, my child. Your power is wild and unrefined, but after tonight, I will unlock your true potential. When Marcelo comes for you, I will be delighted when he tears open your throat and drinks your blood. You will then feast on his, and tomorrow you will wake from death under my control."

Umaq stepped out of the ring. "Let's make the final preparations, Cessani. Nala'thelx is patrolling the woods, and Sebas will alert us when Marcelo nears."

"Your demon pet owes me a new front door, Umaq," said Cessani. "He didn't have to damage it."

"Don't worry, that was all part of the fun," he replied.

The two continued arguing until their voices disappeared into the trees. The coven also rose from their positions and vanished into the woods, leaving Sybil alone in the clearing. Although the restrictive force had lifted from her body, the ropes still confined her to the pole. At least she could breathe a bit easier.

"Please, Marcelo, do not come hither," she whispered to the starry sky. "I do not wish to see you harmed, and I cannot bear the thought of them using you. Allow them to punish me. Of a truth, I deserve it after everything I have done hitherto since waking from the spell. Yonder descendants were innocent, I realize that forthwith. I am so, so sorry. Shall you ever forgive me?"

Emotional pain greater than Cessani's agonizing potion bore into Sybil. The unbearable ache twisted her insides and ripped her soul. Sorrow melted her will, and guilt crushed her fighting spirit. She had grown into a hollow shell with nothing left. The terrified faces of the descendants and their family members haunted her. An innocent woman lay in a coma, and Sybil had nearly drowned a man in front of his children. She deserved punishment, even welcomed it.

Overhead, a waxing moon drifted in blackness. The Maiden watched, but Sybil didn't deserve a deity's mercy or divine intervention. *Let the gods be silent and ever watchful, and let the nature spirits witness Fate's retribution against me.*

Chapter Seventeen

A Force Stronger Than Magic

Sitting in his parked car south of Salem State University, Marcelo sighed and checked the tracking app on his phone. Late at night, Sybil still hadn't moved from someone's house near Highway 1A on Cleveland Road. He had monitored her location throughout the day and now at this extended visit in a stranger's home. He knew this place didn't belong to one of her targets, as the glowing drop of blood hadn't settled in this area on the paper map.

What was Sybil doing there? Had she performed another location spell to find new descendants?

The dot on the phone map started to move. He fired the engine and pulled onto the road to follow Sybil. The tracking app had become essential; knowing her whereabouts could help Marcelo save her next victim's life.

Given the speed at which the signal traveled, Sybil had evidently gotten into a car with someone. Driving toward Marblehead, Marcelo cursed when the GPS signal from her smartphone vanished. Had she discovered the tracking app and turned it off? More likely her phone had died, but either way he had lost his method of pursuit. Afraid of being spotted, he had lagged too far behind and failed to get a visual on the vehicle. He cursed again, not knowing where they were as he tried to think of what to do next.

He drove around for a few miles in the slim hope he would get lucky and spot Sybil. Continuing into Marblehead on Route 114, or Lafayette Street, Marcelo executed a few random turns in the city. He drove past other vehicles out on late night trips and inspected the passengers. He slowed near pedestrians and searched faces for Sybil. After twenty minutes he cruised by Marblehead High School and realized the effort was a waste of time.

Out of nowhere, an animal scampered across the road in front of the car. Marcelo slammed the brakes and screeched to a halt. Glancing around, he swore he had seen a monkey dart past the headlights. A rock struck his window and cracked it as bizarre laughter sounded in the night.

Marcelo climbed out of the vehicle and dodged another rock thrown at his head. "Hey!" he shouted. "Come show yourself." His heightened senses included excellent night vision, but he didn't see anyone.

"Here! Here!" a high-pitched voice called.

Marcelo whirled. A fluffy brown monkey with a gray mouth and nose jumped up and down on the roof of the BMW. The animal threw another rock. Marcelo caught the projectile and hurled it back at the primate.

The creature shrieked and leapt onto the road. "I give up! I give up!" the monkey wailed.

"Who are you, and what do you want?" Marcelo asked. Clearly this wasn't an ordinary animal, but a supernatural entity carrying a specific purpose.

"I am Sebas," said the monkey. "I serve Umaq, the Betrayer. Sybil! Sybil! You are looking for the witch."

"Tell me where she is!" Marcelo demanded.

He charged forward in a burst of speed. The nimble creature vanished between his outstretched hands and reappeared on the hood of the car.

Sebas laughed into a paw, the sound a shrill squeal. "I won't tell you. But I will show you, silly vampire. Can you keep up?" The primate dashed down the road, its tail waving in the air.

Marcelo jumped back behind the wheel. The tires barked on the asphalt as he threw the BMW into gear and raced after Sebas. The wild, intelligent creature zoomed around a few cars on the street. The drivers honked or hit their brakes in alarm. Marcelo passed the startled traffic and skidded around a corner in a smooth drift. Bathed by the car's headlights, the monkey charged on, its tiny paws a blur on the road.

On West Shore Drive, Sebas veered left and dove into a knot of woods. Marcelo skidded to a stop, then maneuvered the car to the side of the road and jumped out. He sprinted into the thicket, the darkness beneath the canopy no problem for his sharp vision.

Howling, Sebas zig-zagged around trunks and darted over gnarled roots. Marcelo nearly caught up to the primate when he rushed through a wall of bushes and entered a clearing. He stopped in shock. Set in a ring of torches and tied to a large wooden pole, Sybil wilted in her restraints. Her head lolled as though unconscious—or worse.

"Sybil!" Marcelo shouted in alarm. He ran into the circle and a deafening voice boomed in his head.

Undead creature, hear me now! My presence, my command, will make you bow. Your spirit is gone, my day is won. The demon rises with the moon, the sun scorches at the high of noon. Witch blood burns in the darkest hour, take Sybil now for her life you'll devour!

Marcelo collapsed and writhed on the grass. He pressed his hands to his temples and shouted in pain. The powerful voice clawed his mind and gnawed his consciousness. Rusted barbs tore his thoughts. Savage teeth shredded his memories.

Blood tears leaked from his eyes. He squinted and saw five robed individuals approach and kneel next to the torches. He tried to stand, but the world spun and knocked him down again as the voice continued.

The demon submits on a bent knee. The master calls, your will yields to me. Come forth and feast for her blood is sublime. Make her yours, forever across time!

Marcelo's awareness slipped further away. His mind whirled in a void, lost without a purpose. His surroundings disappeared. A thousand skinless, bloody arms groped him. Demons wailed in the darkness, a cacophony of chaos and rabid hunger. Eyes blazing with fire watched him. Fanged mouths snarled and tore at his cognizance until none of Marcelo remained.

A heartbeat woke him. The pulse sounded loud, and its bloody rhythm soothed. Human body heat warmed him. Marcelo rose and looked upon a female lashed to a post. His prey stood helpless, an easy kill.

Disappointment overcame him when he realized no hunt would take place.

He moved closer to the young girl. Her heart thundered and blood rushed through her arteries, an entrancing music and promise of sweet nourishment. Marcelo pressed his body against her. Her warmth offered a loving caress against his cold skin, her flesh smooth and supple. He cupped her face as tears filled light brown eyes.

"Marcelo," she whispered weakly. "Truly, you are stronger than this. Do not allow them to hurt you. I care not what happens to me, but I desire for you to be safe and happy. I am sorry for everything hitherto, but you need to leave forthwith. Break yonder spell, Marcelo. Come back to yourself and flee far away."

He smiled. His prey always begged and offered alternatives in pathetic attempts to escape. He leaned down and opened his mouth. Fangs brushed against the soft skin of her throat.

"Kendrick stands hither, just behind you," she continued. "He hath striven to arrange this entire affair, remember? He is our real enemy. Truly, his yellow eyes haunted my dreams for over three hundred years. Yet you woke me, my darling, and spared me from unending nightmares."

His yellow eyes.

Bits of memory surfaced in the dark void of Marcelo's shattered mind: Spanish Conquistadors, a jungle in the ancient Inca Empire, and a copper-skinned man with yellow eyes. Marcelo had *known* this man. But how…when? The fragments of memory swirled. He struggled to grasp them and throw the pieces back together.

A strange voice called out and fractured his concentration. *Drink her blood! Make her one of your kind!*

Marcelo screamed in the emptiness, kicked and clawed at an invisible entity that tried to command him. "Shut the hell up!" he shouted at the demon soul trapped inside him.

It's not me doing this, you idiot, the demonic entity retorted. *Your memories are also mine, and that girl is right. You—we—are under a spell by that crazed Inca from our past. This is infuriating! As much as I'd love to tear open that girl's throat, I will not submit to that man's control again. Break free of the curse, Marcelo!*

Marcelo didn't know if he could tolerate this anymore. His confused, devastated mind had fallen under a relentless assault from all angles. First, a mysterious voice had directed him, the powerful words impossible to ignore. Then the strange girl's soft, cajoling words pleaded and spoke of a common enemy. Lastly, the demon soul howled in a black rage and also mentioned a mutual adversary.

An Inca.

Marcelo strained through a mental barrier and managed to grasp a few more shards of memory. He sewed them together, and they broke apart. He tied the recollections together, and they shattered. Struggling, he welded the memories together and held them firm in his grip.

"Yes, Marcelo, keep striving!" the girl said in desperation.

Do not give up, you fool human! the demon soul urged.

The girl and the monster inside had provided Marcelo invaluable clues about a shared enemy. Yellow eyes. Inca. Memories and emotion blasted through a dam and flooded his consciousness. Recalling more detail, his self-awareness clashed against the strong magic clouding his mind. Patrolling the jungle. Demons and a portal of fire. Death. A withered, yellow-eyed Inca shouting in a foreign tongue…

…the man who had killed Marcelo and bonded the demon spirit to his corpse!

"Come back to me," the girl's voice echoed in the nothing.

Run, you moron! the demon hollered.

In a wild hallucination, Marcelo charged toward a distant light source—an escape. Black, gnarled hands grasped his wrists and ankles to hold him back. He writhed and summoned all the strength he could, desperate to reach the way out.

"I want to be with you," a sweet, familiar voice whispered in his ear.

And I despise you, the demon soul added. *This isn't over yet, be on your guard!*

Invigoration surged in Marcelo. He thrashed, pushed, and pulled against the restraining hands. Fingers broke and wrists snapped as he jerked free. He burst forward in a shout and sprinted down a dark tunnel, then threw himself into the light.

Marcelo tasted blood. He blinked, and for a moment had no idea where he stood. His face lay buried in someone's neck. Fangs barely penetrated the person's skin in tiny punctures. He pulled back in confusion and stared at his beloved Sybil, the source of the passionate whisper.

"Sybil! My head…I…what's going on?"

"Impossible!" a furious voice shouted behind them. "How did he break the enchantment? My spell preparation was flawless. I waited hundreds of years for nothing!"

Marcelo turned around. A horrific manifestation from five hundred years ago stood before him—the black-haired, yellow-eyed man from the jungle. Still dazed from the spell's influence, he shook his head to clear the fuzziness. As if from a dream, he recalled Sybil's and the demon's words from moments ago. This Inca was also Kendrick, the same man who had tormented Sybil during the Salem Witch Trials. Everything snapped into place as Marcelo recovered.

In many fairy tales, it is love that breaks the curse and saves the day. However, it took a volatile mixture of adoration and conflict to shatter Kendrick's spell. Sybil and Marcelo desired to be together, yet at the same time had nearly killed each other. Also a victim in this chaos, the demonic spirit's abhorrence of Kendrick—and of Marcelo—acted as a catalyst to help break the magic. Who would have thought this odd combination of torn feelings, broken hearts, and opposing motivations would do the trick.

Mortified at almost taking Sybil's life, Marcelo placed a hand over the blood on her neck to check the bite wound. "I can't believe I did this to you. Are you all right?"

"I fare well, but danger stands hither," she said. "I cannot fight forthwith."

"Then let's get you out of here." He reached behind her to break the cords, but a spell struck his back and engulfed it in fire. Marcelo clenched his teeth and staggered away. He dodged another blazing sphere as it sailed past his head.

The witches at the edge of the circle gripped their torches. The fires roared bright with magic. Gesturing in unison, the robed group launched more fiery projectiles at Marcelo. In a burst of speed, he darted around the sizzling spheres as they appeared to slow. His feet blurred over the grass. His body hissed through the air as one by one he knocked the witches unconscious before they had an opportunity to defend themselves.

Marcelo tore off his shirt and beat out the flames, then spotted Kendrick moving away across the clearing. Pumped up from battle, he glared at the man and yelled, "You wanted the demon inside of me? Now you have him!"

An elderly woman beside Kendrick turned and fled into the woods. Marcelo ignored her and raced across the grass toward the old man.

"Nala'thelx, go kill that bothersome vampire!" Kendrick shouted as he bolted into the trees.

A towering demon with a skinless, vein-covered body broke through the foliage at the edge of the meadow and charged. Marcelo met the creature at full speed and tackled it to the ground in a thunderous, bone-jarring collision. Straddling the big demon, he hammered a fist into the monster's face and cracked bone, but Nala'thelx barely flinched.

Growling, the beast flipped Marcelo over and bit down on his shoulder. In retaliation, Marcelo grabbed the back of the monster's head and underneath its jaw, trying to twist and snap its neck. The creature wrestled free and rained powerful fists into Marcelo's face and ribs. Snarling, the demon lifted the vampire and hurled him through the air. Helpless, Marcelo could only watch a tree approach until he slammed against it and cracked the trunk.

Nala'thelx wasted no time in continuing the assault. Marcelo tried to stand, but a massive cloven hoof stomped on his bitten shoulder. Pinned to the ground, he struggled as Nala'thelx reached up and snapped off a thick branch from the tree. The powerful demon's howl shook the leaves as it slammed the branch into Marcelo's chest.

The makeshift weapon ripped apart undead flesh and crunched through his sternum. Marcelo ceased struggling, his arms and legs heavy and limp. A deep exhaustion smothered him. His half-lidded eyes fell on Sybil far across the clearing where she writhed in her bonds. Her mouth screamed unheard words.

Marcelo had failed Sybil. Would he ever see her again? Still capable of human sentiment, emotional pain radiated from his long dead heart. Love, regret, and sorrow saturated his core. His vision blurred in red tears of blood.

The horrid demon peeled back its lips in a sadistic smile. "Now for the witch," Nala'thelx rumbled as he turned away.

Chapter Eighteen

Like Fine Wine

Watching the horrific battle, Sybil screamed when Nala'thelx pierced Marcelo's chest using the tree branch. She thrashed against the ropes holding her tight. The cords cut her wrists and ankles after each jerk of her body.

"This cannot be," she wailed. "Marcelo!"

"Be still," a familiar voice suddenly said behind her. "Let me cut you free."

"Grace?" Sybil asked in astonishment. "Flee forthwith, yonder monster is coming!"

"I've seen worse," Grace replied as she worked the ropes off with a knife. "My boss at work is uglier and meaner than that demon."

The restraints fell away, and Grace immediately shoved a stack of herbs into Sybil's mouth. "Chew this and swallow. It will remove the dampening effects of Cessani's potion."

Sybil ground the remedy between her teeth and nearly spit out the acrid concoction. Gagging, she swallowed the herbs and felt as if a wet blanket had been removed from her body. The thick fog in her head cleared. She barely had a second to kiss Grace on the cheek before Nala'thelx drew near.

"Now smash that monstrous thing," Grace said before running toward the woods. "Let me take care of Marcelo."

Fearing for Grace's safety and resisting the urge to run to Marcelo, Sybil held her ground as the demon stopped at the edge of the circle and roared.

"Umaq is a fool for wasting his time with an insignificant witch like you," Nala'thelx growled. "All he ever needed was me. To prove it, I'll bring him your head and the vampire's impaled heart."

Sybil looked past the demon and at Marcelo's unmoving form. Small flashes of light burst beneath the tree as Grace worked magic. Could she really save him? Sybil trembled in effort to keep her grief subdued. She wanted to cry, but similar to when Constance died, she pushed all emotion aside and became *nothing*. Only a cold hollow remained in her gut, her humanity frozen as her temples pulsed in rage.

Sybil gazed at the unconscious witches lying on the turf. She snapped her fingers, and the five torch posts ripped from the ground. Thrusting a palm at Nala'thelx, the flaming poles sailed toward the demon and skewered his body, the fires hissing and snuffing out.

Howling, the skinless monster staggered back and dropped to a knee. He pulled the stakes from his worm-covered body, then stood and bounded toward Sybil.

"Weak!" the demon shouted.

Reaching down, she tore out several strands of grass. Throwing the blades in the air, the grass wove into a long, thick braid and spun toward Nala'thelx. The weave wrapped around the monster's thick neck and tightened. The demon stumbled and choked, his breath ragged. He managed to wriggle a sharp claw between the cord and his neck to cut the braid loose.

The demon swept its muscled arm, and Sybil dove on the ground to dodge. Nala'thelx then gripped the large wooden column she had been tied to and pulled it from the earth. Using the post as a weapon, he charged and unleashed a series of swings and thrusts, trying to pound her into the meadow.

Sybil rolled away from the falling column. The hard blow quivered the earth in a near miss. She scrambled to her feet and ran, her hands up. Miniature bolts of lightning sparkled on her palms, then spread to her arms and down the rest of her body. Electricity hummed and crackled around her in a tight cocoon. Nala'thelx swung the wooden post and hit nothing as Sybil teleported across the clearing in a loud crash of thunder.

The monster glanced about in confusion. Sybil only had a moment for her next spell. With the lightning still active over her body, she grabbed the writhing, flashing tendrils and wrapped them into a large sparkling ball. *"Storms from high, split the sky, this cloudless night defy. Display your might, dance so bright, lightning strike this demon from my sight!"*

She lifted the sizzling ball and threw it into the air. The compressed lightning buzzed at high speed toward Nala'thelx. The demon chopped down at the spell with the huge club, but the lightning sphere sliced through the wood and plowed into the monster. The demon's upper body exploded in a shower of rotten flesh and bone. Gray worms spewed everywhere. Still intact, his lower torso and legs wobbled a few steps before collapsing in the grass.

Sybil looked around the area, but Umaq and Cessani were long gone. Two of the injured witches moaned and began to stir. Leaving them, she ran to Marcelo and realized Grace had left at some point. Sybil's heart thundered in anticipation as hope and fear churned in her stomach.

"Marcelo!" she called, kneeling next to him.

The branch had been removed from his body. Grace's magic had healed some of the gaping wound, but it appeared a full recovery would take time and more spell-work.

Marcelo opened his eyes. "That demon was strong, but stupid," he said weakly. "He nicked my heart instead of impaling it. Usually only fire hurts, but the small slice on my heart caused enough damage to put me down. A fraction more to the left and I'd be dead."

Now Sybil allowed herself to cry. She threw herself onto him and ignored his grunt of pain as she covered his face in kisses.

"Truly, let us not leave each other ever again," she said between sobs. "I am sorry for everything, Marcelo. It is well if you do not forgive me. I just—"

"Enough," he said quietly, sitting up in effort. "You've been through hell and nobody's perfect, least of all me. I've already forgiven you, Sybil. We have much to discuss, but for now I'm glad to be alive and even happier to be with you."

Foliage rustled off in the distance as running footsteps approached. Grace had gone into the woods and returned. She bent over, hands on her knees and out of breath. "You two look sweet and I wish I had a camera, but Umaq has gone into Cessani's house and they're doing some kind of spell. There are all sorts of weird lights flashing from inside."

The ground rocked and trees swayed in a sudden, violent quake. Sybil and the others cried out in surprise and fell. Holding on to each other and moving carefully, the group shuffled to the center of the clearing as tremors toppled several trees around the perimeter.

From beyond the woods in the direction of Cessani's house, a bright column of light exploded into the sky. The wide shaft stretched to the heavens, and a powerful hum radiated from the glow. Black bolts of lightning crackled around the pillar. Tendrils of fire blazed fierce in random patterns up and down the illuminated column.

The shaking stopped. Heard over the loud buzz from the light, terrifying, otherworldly sounds grew everywhere. Demonic howls split the night. Guttural roars, growls, and hunger-filled cries seemed to rattle the town.

"Something comes hither!" Sybil shouted.

Along the tree line, foliage snapped and grass rustled as several horrid creatures broke through and sprinted on all fours across the meadow. Long, sparse hair on the demons' gray backs fluttered. Sharp, bony protrusions marked their muscled bodies. Grasping claws ripped up clods of earth with each long stride. Elongated snouts dripped saliva between crooked teeth, and three eyes glared on each head.

"Get ready for a fight!" Grace called, standing in a defensive posture.

"Wait, they're ignoring us," said Marcelo.

The mob of demons continued past the clearing and tore into the trees on the opposite side.

"They're rallying toward that light where Umaq and Cessani are," Grace observed.

"Let's chase after them," Marcelo replied. He started to run, then faltered and uttered a low groan.

Sybil approached and looked at the ugly wound in his chest. The puncture showed improvement, but the injury to his heart still bothered him.

"We shall retreat to safety," she said in concern. "You look terrible, I warrant. Handsome, but terrible."

"This may be our last chance to stop Kendrick, Umaq, or whatever his name is," he said through a grimace. "Grace gave me a nice dose of healing, and I can make it. We have to go after him, Sybil. You've waited over three hundred years for this."

Apprehension for Marcelo's wellbeing didn't fade, but Sybil knew he spoke true. Even though Umaq's plan had failed tonight, the man had grown alarmingly strong over the centuries and had recruited powerful allies. The dangerous situation was far from over. The proof lay with endless demons awakening everywhere and in that crazy light blasting into the sky.

Sybil gazed into the severe determination in Marcelo's green eyes. She also knew it would take more than a tree branch to slow her dear vampire. Grace offered a firm nod, courage and resolve stamped on her face. After a return nod to her friend, Sybil broke into a run and led the others into the woods.

Moving through the trees, glimpses of the bright column peeked through the leafy canopy as Sybil headed toward the source of the illumination. Finally leaving the woods, she encountered a chaotic scene in the small neighborhood where Cessani lived.

In a sea of twinkling red and blue lights, police cars jammed the street. Helicopters buzzed around the huge glowing shaft protruding through the roof of Cessani's home. Loud gunfire from the cops cracked the air. Bullets whizzed toward a flood of demons charging toward the house. The panicked residents screamed while shoving their families inside cars to escape.

"We shall go to yonder cottage," Sybil called over the noise. "The demons seem more concerned with getting to Umaq and Cessani than attacking anyone."

The frenzied demons had shattered windows as they plowed inside the home. As if in a trance, the creatures ignored Sybil and the others while she led them through an opening and into a huge parlor.

The interior of the residence lay in disaster. Smashed furniture, ripped carpet, shattered tile, broken plaster, and splintered wood sat everywhere. Like moths to a flame, the demons scampered through the debris and leapt into the light source, a large glowing ball in the center of the parlor. The bright pillar of energy grew from the sphere and had broken through the ceiling up into the sky. Through the large hole in the roof, Sybil could see one of the helicopters circling.

"It's a portal," Grace remarked. "Look at all these monsters! There's no way we can stop them."

"Umaq is amassing his demon army in Peru, in Machu Picchu," said Sybil. "And he shall summon forth more powerful creatures using the ancient portals at yonder Inca ruins. That is what Cessani claimed, if it be true."

Marcelo went to check the adjacent rooms, then returned shaking his head. "No sign of anyone. They must have escaped with the monsters through the portal, but I wouldn't worry about losing Umaq. If he really went to Machu Picchu, it won't be long before a breaking news report informs the world. The sudden appearance of a demon horde in one of the world's most amazing tourist locations is bound to catch someone's attention."

The gunfire intensified. An explosion shook the street, followed by several shouts.

"It's a war zone out there," said Grace. "Let's get out of here before we're caught by the police and hauled in for questioning."

"Follow me to my car," said Marcelo.

Moving past a snarling demon, Sybil and the others left Cessani's destroyed house and slipped back into the woods. They skirted the edge of the trees and ended up on West Shore Drive near the vehicle. Sybil hopped into the front passenger seat while Grace settled in the back.

Marcelo drove off and jerked the car to the side as two monsters scrambled across the road. Regaining control, he accelerated and sped away from the bedlam. Around town the demons poured out from everywhere. They emerged from parks, schools, and adjacent neighborhoods in a steady stream. Police cars zoomed about, sirens blaring, trying to chase down the creatures and protect the citizens.

Dismay filled Sybil as she gripped the seatbelt and stared out the window. "A great sundry of demons. We must find a way to stop Umaq."

"For now, you two need to regroup and rest," Grace replied. "You and Marcelo have been dropped inside a blender. You are physically, mentally, and emotionally exhausted. Let's go to my house for some hot tea…spiked with plenty of bourbon."

Sybil didn't argue. As much as her desire burned to eliminate Umaq, she really needed time to patch up her mind and body. Not only that, but also to mend her relationship with Marcelo. He had forgiven her, but they still had plenty to talk about to rebuild trust. Only together could the both of them succeed against Umaq.

Chapter Nineteen

Second Wind

The intense light swallowed Umaq. Moments later, he opened his eyes to find himself in old, familiar territory. The portal had taken him to the place of his birth, the great Inca city of Machu Picchu in the country of Peru. He stood in the crumbled remains of the Temple of the Three Windows, aptly named for the three openings in the largest wall constructed from polygonal shaped rocks. A star-filled sky stretched overhead, the original grass, branch, and adobe roof long gone.

The window called Kay-Pacha represented the present time or the Earth's surface. Umaq had used this opening to create the portal that connected Machu Picchu to Cessani's house. Bright light filled the window as the lesser demons from Salem and Marblehead continued to pour through. Freed from their long period of dormancy, the creatures spread among the ruins, howling and sniffing at everything.

Between the demons, Cessani stepped through the portal and onto the dirt floor. She dragged an old trunk and glanced about wearing a look of irritation. "You could have given me a few more minutes to gather my things, Umaq. I had to leave a lot behind."

"Welcome to my home," said Umaq. "No need to worry. The portal will close soon, but your coven can bring the rest of your materials when they arrive by plane."

"And where am I supposed to sleep? This place is a mess."

"Hey, you're talking about my ancestry, have some respect," he replied, amused by the witch's modern expectations. "These minor demons running about aren't just foot soldiers. With their strength and ease of manipulation, they'll soon rebuild Machu Picchu to be as magnificent and impenetrable as it ever was. You will have a good roof over your head, Cessani, and much comfort. Take a minute to look around and use your imagination."

Leaving the witch, Umaq walked past a lone pillar that used to support the roof of the Temple of the Three Windows. He stepped into the darkened Sacred Plaza, an area that once represented the political center of the urban district, and where various celebrations and festivals occurred.

Atop a large hill and above zigzagging flights of steps sat Intihuatana, the religious stone monument whose name signified "where the sun is tied." Powered by ley lines, the immediate area around Intihuatana tingled with enormous, mystical energy. Ceremonies honoring the sun god, Inti, used to take place at the stone shrine.

Umaq clenched his fists as a bitter memory stirred. Before his hatred for the sun god developed, he used to weave magic in honor of Inti. His spells called for a plentiful crop during harvest time, for the sun to shine bright so it would nourish the produce, or to burn less when rain grew scarce. But when the sun failed to bless the crop or its heat scorched the harvest, the Inca citizens didn't blame Inti—their ridicule and hatred fell on Umaq.

His continued devotion to the solar deity only resulted in curses and stones thrown from the Incas. Umaq's wounded mind, shattered feelings, and bruised flesh had turned his soul black. The failure to aid his people constantly reminded him how faith in Inti only brought misery and ruin. Those hard lessons proved that success would only be achieved through his own efforts. No more relying on scarcely observed and unpredictable deities. No more spellcrafting in their honor or pining for divine inspiration.

The old gods had grown obsolete; only Umaq the Betrayer remained. With his demons, he would eradicate Inti to blight the sun's light and mold the world beneath a smothering darkness.

"There you are," Cessani called, interrupting his thoughts. "I looked around a bit, and this place has huge potential. I get goosebumps from the stored energy here. The ley lines are some of the strongest I've ever felt." She gestured to the towering bulk of Huayna Picchu, the sharp-peaked mountain overlooking Machu Picchu. "I've read all about the Temple of the Moon up there. I can't wait to see it and get set up inside. What a beautiful and commanding location to call on Mama Quilla."

Umaq's anger returned in a flash. "The Inca moon goddess won't help you, and neither will the Maiden. What did I say about relying on the old gods? Forget about those useless deities and trust in yourself. We have a lot of work to do and don't have time for futile ritual and worship. Starting tomorrow, this entire place will undergo a massive transformation. The world's attention will be on us, and they'll try to tear down what we've started. We need to summon our allies and recruit new ones." He placed his hands on her shoulders. "I need you, Cessani. Not some dusty lunar goddesses who only care about themselves."

Cessani smiled in the bright starlight. Her knowing look and mysterious eyes made it difficult to read her expression. If Umaq suspected she posed any threat to him, he would have plunged his hand into her chest and ripped out any bad intentions from her heart.

"You shouldn't worry so much, Umaq," she replied. "Mama Quilla and the Maiden don't hold anything against you. Consider us gossiping ladies on the mountaintop, that's all. I want this to happen just as much as you do, remember? Witches have lost all respect and status over the centuries, and I'm here to change that. My coven will assist you. But the moon goddesses are mine to deal with, not yours."

Even if Cessani spoke true, Umaq considered impaling her chest just out of spite. But he really did need the old witch and her coven. She had proven to be a formidable ally, and so far, he didn't have a reason to distrust the woman.

"Fine," he said at last. "Just do your thing up in the Temple of the Moon, not down here in the city."

A distant whistle suddenly blew. Umaq and Cessani hurried back to the Temple of the Three windows to find the source. The glowing portal in the Kay-Pacha opening had vanished; all the lesser demons had arrived. Umaq peered through the gap and down at the Central Plaza, a wide field of grass that divided the

Sacred Plaza, temples, and Intihuatana from the other districts on the far side of the city.

The whistle blew again, and three flashlights carried by nighttime security bobbed through the grass. These uniformed men had been expected, as the ancient tourist site required protection from thieves or vandals in the night. Demons emerged from nooks and shadows between the abandoned structures. Their feral howls echoed in the ruins. Soon the guards' screams filled the Central Plaza as the creatures mauled the security team.

"That won't be the last time blood is spilled here," Umaq said from the window. "But no one can stop us. We've come too far to fail."

"You still sound confident after having your centuries-old plan crushed," Cessani replied, sitting down on the trunk she had brought. "So what happens now?"

"Losing Sybil doesn't mean an end to my goal. It simply means I'm without a strong general to lead my army." He pointed to another of the three windows in the temple wall. "That's Uku-Pacha, which means the underground or inner life. I'll create a new portal there that connects to the netherworld, and the greatest of demons will come through at my bidding. Once I'm ready, I will challenge Inti and annihilate him. The celestial energy will then darken to further strengthen my grip on the world."

He studied Cessani for a moment. "With the mystical balance shifted, that also means a more powerful moon," he added. "Should make your lunar deities happy, I suppose."

"Of course," she agreed, displaying another mysterious smile. "It will also please the witches who follow them."

Not wanting to waste more time fretting over Cessani's petty intentions, Umaq glanced up to where the sacred stone, Intihuatana, lay on the hill beneath the starry heavens. Soon a god would fall, and nothing would deter his own satisfaction while fulfilling his ultimate revenge.

Chapter Twenty

Amends

Standing on Grace's porch, Sybil wrapped her dear friend in a tight hug. She buried her face in the older woman's neck and didn't want to let go. The morning sun bathed the yard in warm light. Birds chirped and fluttered between trees. A dog barked in the distance. Sybil and Marcelo had spent the night at Grace's house after talking for hours over tea and bourbon. Now it was time to leave.

"I am in your debt, Grace," said Sybil. "If not for you, I would still be tied to yonder pole and shredded to pieces." She pulled back and cupped the woman's motherly face. "You conceive my story forthwith, and I apologize for my lies and deceit beforehand. Truly, you are an amazing witch, and I would love to be part of your coven."

Enthusiasm lit Grace's blue eyes, her smile wide. "Oh, that would be so wonderful! No fancy initiation ceremony necessary. I believe we experienced enough pomp and magic last night while fighting for our lives. Consider yourself a lifetime member."

Sybil laughed and hugged her friend again. She would miss Grace, but this certainly wasn't the last time they would see each other. A reunion proved inevitable as the three of them had vowed to battle Umaq and Cessani together.

"Shall you be safe?" Sybil asked. "All the demons left and Umaq hath gone forth, but I shall never stop worrying about you."

Grace gently squeezed Sybil's shoulders. "I'll be fine, dear. This is witch territory and I have many connections from here to Boston, some human and others supernatural. I'll keep an eye on things in Salem while you and Marcelo drum up some allies in California."

Wearing clothing to protect him from the sun, Marcelo stepped through the screen door and onto the porch. "I just hope some of my old associates will help us against Umaq." He adjusted the scarf and hat Grace had provided. "Fickle is the best way to describe them."

He exchanged a hug with Grace and planted a kiss on her cheek. "I am also in your debt, Grace. Thank you for ripping the tree branch from my body and patching me up."

"Think nothing of it," she said. "I wish you luck in your recruitment back home. You two watch your backs. Cessani has a much larger network than mine from here to the west coast. She and Umaq know you still pose a threat. Be safe, and don't hesitate to call me for anything."

Grace walked them to the car. Sybil hugged her friend again, then climbed into the passenger seat. She and Marcelo had a long day ahead of them. Tonight, their flight would take them to San Luis Obispo in California. But first, some critical tasks remained in Salem. Marcelo waved, and they drove off toward their first stop of the day at North Shore Medical Center.

Walking the brightly lit corridors of the hospital, desolation wilted Sybil's shoulders and her heart grew heavy. Marcelo's supportive arm around her did little to quell the anxiety roiling inside her. After checking in at the nurse's station, Sybil entered Elizabeth Sanford's room in the intensive care ward.

Elizabeth was the descendant Sybil had drained a large amount of life energy from. Since that day, the poor woman had lain in a coma. Stuffed animals, flowers, and cards sat on a table in a corner of the room. Machinery hummed and hissed. Elizabeth did not deserve to be in this condition, and Sybil had come here to remedy that.

She took out a charm bag she had made and slipped it beneath the pillow. A pinch of rosemary, willow tree bark, myrrh oil, and quartz crystals filled the velvet sack. Earlier, Sybil had also enhanced the healing properties of the ingredients by using candle magic. Glancing at the door to make sure no one besides Marcelo was around, she placed a hand over Elizabeth's chest and closed her eyes.

Rich green fog drifted from Sybil's hand and seeped into the woman. The invigorated, mystical vapor would recharge Elizabeth's strength and vitality. A few more days and the charm bag would do the rest. The woman would awake refreshed and healthy, her mind, body, and spirit restored.

Sybil added a second item to the table—a long letter of apology. Elizabeth would never know who Sybil was or why this happened, but the handwritten message and the healing spell signified the least she could do.

Nodding to Marcelo, they exited the room and departed the hospital for their next destination.

Marcelo pulled up to the post office on Margin Street. Sybil stepped out of the car with two more letters of apology, one for the man she tried to drown in Boston and the other for the family she had attacked in that city as well. As with Elizabeth, none of the victims would ever know anything about Sybil or why these assaults occurred, but perhaps the genuine remorse in her letters could help ease their minds and bring those families some peace.

Her tasks done, Marcelo then drove toward a place where Sybil hoped to find some peace of her own. South of the Peabody Essex Museum on Charter Street stood the Salem Witch Trials Memorial. Marcelo had told her about this place, but an initial fear that her lust for vengeance might return prevented her from visiting. However, overcoming that fear represented a primary step for her emotional and spiritual recovery. She couldn't fight Umaq and help others without helping herself first.

Holding Marcelo's gloved hand in a tight grip, she took a deep breath and approached the memorial, a simple yet beautiful courtyard that contained a field of grass and five black locust trees. A handcrafted, low granite wall enclosed the area on three sides. Protruding from the wall, twenty stone benches held the inscribed name of the accused during the witch trials, and the date and method of each execution.

Feeling numb and detached from reality, Sybil walked slowly along the cement path that ran between the granite wall and the grass area. Bridget Bishop, Elizabeth Howe, Rebecca Nurse, and Sarah Good were some of the twenty victims etched on the benches. Her mouth grew dry, and her heart pounded in her ears. The more Sybil read and the further she strode, the closer she arrived to one name in particular.

Constance Chandler, hanged, June 10th, 1692.

Sybil gasped, unprepared for the inscription's impact. Lightheaded, she nearly swooned before Marcelo steadied her. She lowered to her knees and placed unsteady hands on the granite bench showing Constance's name. This location was not the young woman's actual burial site—that remained unknown—but the memorialization and solemn atmosphere made Sybil cry.

"I have arrived hither, my dear beloved," she whispered. "Truly, my heart misses you so much. I shall always remember our time together in yonder little cottage with the thatch roof. You were my coven, my life." She wiped her eyes and traced the etched name with her finger. "Years agone you always said I took care of you, but forthwith I need you to watch over me. This new world is so large and terrifying, I warrant. I lost my way and only conceived darkness and despair. Please, show me how to be strong and to do what is right."

Sybil stood and gazed down at the bench. She had mourned her mother for three years after arriving in Salem Village. But with Constance, her death remained fresh in Sybil's mind after waking from her sleep. Twice, she had been denied the chance to properly bury her loved ones. She envisioned her mother's name, Olivia, etched into the stone as well. This emotional moment in the silent memorial provided the opportunity for closure, to say goodbye to her mother and friend.

Sybil closed her eyes and sighed. "I waited over three hundred years to say farewell. Be at peace, dear Constance, and beloved Mother. I love you both very much."

She turned to find Marcelo standing down the path, his head lowered in respect. Grace had given him an old boonie hat, a bright colored scarf, and large sunglasses as defense from the sun.

Sybil approached him and smiled, her heart light and mind much clearer. "Your appearance is silly, but handsome, my vampire knight. Thank you for being with me, Marcelo. Of a truth, I do not believe I could have come hither alone."

Without the need for words, he took her in his arms and she snuggled against his undead body. Not warm, but uplifting and comfortable in its *reality*. Wrapped in silence, they returned to the car and headed for the Hawthorne Hotel. Upon arriving, she threw herself on the bed in exhaustion and napped beside Marcelo until the time came to head for the airport.

***

The flight to the west coast arrived in San Luis Obispo just before midnight. Instead of apprehension over flying, Sybil had been thrilled by the journey. The physical sensations on her body, the night view of twinkling lights below, and even the snacks provided an emotional experience.

After collecting their luggage and walking to the parking lot, Marcelo expressed his excitement to finally have his blue Aston Martin Rapide back. Sybil loved the car the moment she saw it. She made him promise to teach her how to drive it one day. After hesitating for several moments, he agreed.

Beneath a star-filled sky, Sybil enjoyed the beautiful ride to Avila Beach. Marcelo pulled into the driveway of his home and brought the suitcases inside, then provided a tour. The modern accommodations astounded her. Attractive, polished wood flooring and plush furniture filled the living room. The gas fireplace and huge flat screen television elated her when she thought of watching *moovys*. Exquisite tile and smooth granite counters decorated the kitchen. Gorgeous marble and gilded mirrors adorned the bathrooms. Soft carpet, lovely wood bureaus, and an amazing king bed sat in the master bedroom.

"We'll have to buy food for the house," Marcelo said, his expression odd. "I haven't done that in years. It feels weird just saying it."

Sybil laughed. "Truly, thank you for being considerate of my human needs." She flopped on the sofa. "You still owe me a telling of your story. All I conceive is that you dwelled in Spain. My time as the *Sleeping Beauty* witch, as you put it, hath ended. Thus, I shall listen to your words. Just who are you, Marcelo Abana Flores?"

Marcelo moved to the sofa and cuddled Sybil as they melted into the cushions. "Aren't you tired? It's late and we can talk in the morning."

"I do not wish to miss another special moment together," she replied. "We have striven through so much with no time to truly speak about each other's lives. It would please me to learn more about yours."

"Then I'll tell you my story," he began. "But first there's something you must know about Umaq. With all of the chaos that's happened, I didn't have a chance to mention this before and I'm still shocked. Umaq is the one who made me a vampire. I didn't know that my murderer and your tormenter were the same person until you helped me break free from his spell."

Sybil froze. "How…how can this be? Truly, that is too much coincidence. I warrant it hath something to do with why Umaq toiled so to bring us hither."

"You're right. It had everything to do with his plan of having me turn you into his puppet. Umaq is a master demon summoner, and as a result, I'm not a normal vampire. That's part of my story, so buckle up and hear me out. I'd offer you a snack, but I don't have any."

"You are an awful host, I warrant," she said, shifting to make herself more comfortable. "Now start talking forthwith."

Chapter Twenty-One

Peruvian Jungle, 1532

Marcelo didn't want to kill anyone. He wanted to go back home to Spain and eat *paella* with his mother. He missed her so much. But here across the Atlantic Ocean in a strange land he had scarcely heard of, he had his orders from the Spanish Conquistador, Francisco Pizarro: *Hunt the natives down, and eliminate them.*

Marcelo held his sword in a sweaty, gloved hand. The bulky, round shield hung gripped in the other. In the jungle heat, the heavy armor wrapping his torso felt like a brick oven. He pushed further into the thick foliage and again thought of his mother.

You are eighteen today, my beloved son. A young man in the army. Come back home soon. I'll make you paella with the white fish and little shrimps you love so much.

She had said those words on the day he boarded the large vessel and set sail toward the New World alongside the other Conquistadors.

There are riches to be won across the ocean, young soldado! Pizarro had said. But Marcelo didn't care about the gold, minerals, and other valuable things the native Incas had. He wanted to leave them in peace so they could eat whatever food they enjoyed with their mothers.

A muffled cry broke his thoughts. The bushes ahead rustled. Another muted wail floated to him in the jungle. Sword raised, he used the weapon to push aside the thick vegetation. His breath caught when he revealed a young native woman and her baby crouched on the ground. The woman had her hand pressed over the baby's mouth in an attempt to stifle the infant's cries.

Shock stunned Marcelo. He felt terrified, but not for himself. If any of the other *soldados* approached, they would certainly capture this woman and her babe. Or perhaps do something worse. A hundred thoughts raced in his mind. Yet through the panic, he was able to observe intriguing details of the Inca and her child.

On the way across the ocean as the ship pitched up and down on the waves, Marcelo had tried to ignore his nausea by asking the other troops about the local culture. Some of the older veterans had been to the New World before, and from them Marcelo had learned about the Incas.

The distraught woman wore an ankle-length tunic of fine, soft cloth woven from the wool of a young alpaca, an animal native to these parts. The cloth was called cumbi, a fabric valued as much as gold. Being a person of wealth, she also wore a dyed, colorful sash covered by discs of gold and precious stones around her waist.

She spoke in a rush of words, but Marcelo could only shake his head. "I don't understand," he told her in Castilian. "You and your baby need to run far away from here."

The bushes to his left stirred. An Inca male dressed in a cumbi tunic split the foliage and charged at Marcelo. He failed to raise the shield in time. The native man slammed a stone into the side of Marcelo's head, and he lost consciousness.

***

Sometime later, he woke up in pain. His head throbbed and body ached, but the agony hadn't roused him—the sensation of being dragged across the turf did. Someone had a firm grip on his wrist while hauling him by the arm across the jungle floor. Marcelo no longer wore armor, and his weapons were gone. Dirt, leaves, and twigs scraped his body. The cotton shirt and trousers he had worn beneath the armor grew soiled and torn.

Weak and disoriented, he lolled his head back and glanced at the native Inca who dragged him, a different man than the one who had attacked him with the stone. In the shafts of afternoon sunlight poking through the jungle canopy, Marcelo saw the back of a copper-skinned, black-haired old man. The individual moved steadily and had strength that defied his thin body. The stranger seemed to care little for Marcelo's condition. That fact, along with the man's unnatural strength, gave him the feeling that this would not be a friendly encounter.

He tried to stand and jerk his arm free. The Inca whirled, and Marcelo halted in terror. The stranger's eyes had no pupils or irises. Only an ugly, sour yellow filled his sockets. Sun-darkened skin and hard wrinkles dominated his face. He squinted as if not able to see well, then spoke an odd word.

Sudden pain exploded in Marcelo's head. He fell to his knees, half-conscious. The old man resumed dragging the young *soldado* away.

Groaning, Marcelo woke again on a dirt floor and opened his eyes in a strange hut. Night loomed through a hole in the middle of the ceiling. Foliage and branches had been lashed together to form crude walls and a roof. A fire roared in the center of the chamber. The old man from before squatted in front of the blaze. Mumbling in a native tongue, he threw purple powder onto the flames and the fire crackled and grew.

Still dizzy and weak, Marcelo crawled away from the flames and pressed against the wall. He spotted the door on the other side of the fire. Standing, he immediately collapsed after an invisible blow cracked him on the kneecaps. He hugged his throbbing knees and glared at his captor's withered, smiling face.

"Let me go!" Marcelo shouted.

The man turned back to the fire. He threw some leaves into the inferno and shouted in a commanding voice. A terrifying scream erupted from the blaze. Despite the suffocating heat, Marcelo shivered at the sound, and goose bumps peppered his skin.

A blackened, oily arm thrust out of the dancing flames. Claw-tipped fingers slammed onto the floor to grip the soil and pull itself forward. A misshapen head with six slanted eyes and no nose emerged from the fire. A gray torso followed and two huge, leathery wings draping on its wide back. The horned creature struggled to free itself from the inferno, its grotesque face twisted in pain and effort.

Horrified, Marcelo's blood turned to ice and his muscles froze. He would have screamed except his throat seized. Rooted to the ground, he could hardly move or breathe.

The old man yelled at the monster. He gestured wildly and threw more purple powder onto the flames. The creature roared in agony, its movements strained and slow. The demon finally pulled itself all the way out of the fire and lay on the dirt, panting. Its veiny wings drooped in exhaustion.

The strange Inca was some sort of powerful *bruja*. He fumbled around on a table for a thin piece of leather and scribbled symbols on it using a piece of charcoal. Poor eyesight kept his face close to the parchment. He appeared agitated, his strokes using the writing tool forceful and careless. Rolling up the leather, he threw it onto the table and paced the room, mumbling.

The monster made a gurgling sound in its throat. Marcelo knew the creature was dying, but that didn't make him feel any safer with the crazy, spell-casting Inca in the hut. The man stepped to the demon and nudged its shoulder. He spoke a few rhythmic words, something like a chant, then pointed at Marcelo.

The demonic creature started to crawl toward him. Now Marcelo did scream, a wild cry of disbelief, bewilderment, and madness. Still lying on the ground, he kicked the beast on the side of its head and tried to stand. A blast of pain erupted on his knees again and he fell.

Jagged claws punctured Marcelo's calf, and he hollered. He attempted to fight back with his other leg, but the monster grabbed his ankle and sank its sharp teeth into his thigh. His fists pounded the demon's multi-eyed face, but the creature hardly flinched. Through tears, Marcelo glanced toward the old man. Squinting, the Inca took notes and observed under a studious expression.

Comprehension dawned and rage burst inside Marcelo. This was just an experiment for the man, an insane test to see how much control he could exert over the demon. Marcelo's anger boiled over, and his fear vanished. He reached down and wrapped his hands around the prone creature's throat. Gritting his teeth in effort, he squeezed and realized this might be the only move that would save him.

It seemed to work. The monster moved slower as it lay partially on top of Marcelo. Its attack grew less intense while it struggled. The foul beast's jaw opened and snapped shut in a loud click of teeth. All six of its eyes closed. The creature's body fell limp and pressed Marcelo into the dirt.

A moment later, a thunderous growl suddenly rumbled in the demon's chest. With renewed force, the beast's blackened arm lashed out. Long claws tore open Marcelo's abdomen. The pain burned like coals in his gut. Adrenaline and panic fueled his strength as he pushed the monster off and crawled away, one hand pressed over his midsection. Blood dripped between his fingers and reddened the earthen floor.

Limbs trembling and breath ragged, Marcelo tried to move through the door. Sweat stung his eyes, and his strength faded. He collapsed and looked back. The old Inca stood over the monster while taking more notes. The motionless creature had succumbed, its half-open eyes staring at nothing in death.

The man hurried over to the fire. He dipped a branch into the flames and waved the smoking wood over his head, uttering another chant.

Unable to move, Marcelo sensed life draining from his body. Grief and terror spilled from his eyes in the form of tears. He thought of his mother and of sharing a plate of *paella* with her. He had known being conscripted into the army had its risks, but never did he imagine this would be the way death greeted him—slaughtered by a demon and a crazed old man.

Barely able to keep his eyes open, Marcelo thought his warped mind played tricks on his vision. The smoke from the branch drifted and settled in a specific area of the hut. A form took shape in the haze. After a moment, he recognized the outline of the demon that had crawled out of the fire.

The creature's dead body lay on the ground, but revealed by the smoke, somehow its essence remained. The Inca shouted a command, and the misty demon spirit moved toward Marcelo. Its broad wings, horns, and claws were nothing more than a vague shadow, yet Marcelo's fear returned as if the beast had regained life and renewed its attack.

The smoke-shape enveloped him as he fought for the last few moments of his life. He closed his eyes to a chorus of howling, though he didn't know if it came from him or the demon. Behind his closed lids, light and dark flashed in rapid succession, sickening him. Something screamed. The sound of falling rocks boomed.

Marcelo fell. His limp body tumbled through the air with no end. He opened his eyes and shouted in alarm. Walls of fire roared and crackled all around. Burning tendrils leapt out to slash his body. The smoke-demon fell alongside him, its leathery wings spread. Marcelo wrestled the creature in a furious battle. Loud grunts and howls echoed amid the surrounding inferno.

Your flesh and bone are mine, mortal!

The beast tore Marcelo's chest open, and he cried out. The demon roared in victory and lost its form as the smoke gathered into a large, cloudy ball. The smoke poured into the gaping wound, its essence of malevolence and decay filling Marcelo. He struck the ground in a violent impact and lay stunned.

Someone kicked his shoulder and shouted in a strange language. Marcelo glanced up and found himself in the Inca's makeshift hut. The heat from the fire pit hurt his skin as if it somehow burned hotter. Beneath his hand, he detected every particle of sand, silt, clay, and organic material in the soil. Somewhere outside a waterfall churned faintly, yet he sensed it stood at least a mile away. In the wood smoke, he smelled water, mold spores, and other odd elements drifting overhead.

Other sounds and smells wafted to him from various distances: a bird eating an insect, a piece of fruit falling from a branch, an animal defecating in the grass. In the hut, the old man's sweat and body odor made Marcelo gag.

Disoriented by his overworked senses and from the bizarre hallucination of the smoke-demon, Marcelo realized he lived. He abruptly laughed and inspected his chest and abdomen; no puncture wounds or blood showed. Had everything been a dream? His smile then vanished as reality struck. The demon's body still lay on the ground, and the old man scribbled furiously onto his parchment.

What had happened? How much of this was real…and why did he feel so strange? The Inca waved his arm and began another chant. Marcelo gazed at him in confusion. The man returned a look of utter bewilderment, then stepped closer and renewed his incantation while gesturing. Was he attempting a spell to attack Marcelo, or to control him like he had the demon? The Inca threw down the parchment and shouted in obvious frustration, his face twisted by rage.

The demented man grabbed a knife from the table and lunged at Marcelo in several half-blind strikes. He easily stepped aside to avoid the attack, then slammed a fist into the Inca's face. The assailant crashed to the floor, unmoving. In Marcelo's ultra-sensitive ears, the unconscious man's heart boomed a steady beat and his soft breath roared like a strong wind. None of this made any sense. Having had enough of this nightmare fiasco, Marcelo stepped through the door and into unknown surroundings.

A glimpse of bright stars and a hazy moon showed through a gap in the jungle canopy. Marcelo knew he shouldn't be able to see well in the shadowed underbrush, but crisp details leapt out in his somehow sharpened vision. The makeshift hut stood alone in the deep jungle, no sign of other people or neighbors nearby. From the outside, the shack appeared hastily built in careless effort, as if the crazed Inca had planned only a temporary stay. Surrounded by thick vegetation and no clear path on the jungle floor, the residence seemed far from any town or village.

However, the scent of cooking meat floated to Marcelo from a distance. The noise of a stone mortar and pestle—and murmured conversation—could be heard far away. He headed for the activity in mixed hope and dread. Had he discovered a Conquistador camp, or would he run into more locals?

He jogged for quite some time, dumbfounded by the great distance he'd been able to smell food and hear voices. Still baffled by the night's events, he finally entered a village in a large clearing. All around him, wood and grass structures filled a small community of blazing fire pits and busy Inca natives.

A cacophony of powerful sensations suddenly blasted Marcelo. The fiery stars blinded. Pounding tools deafened him. The surrounding jungle moaned, and the dirt vibrated beneath his feet. Voices rushed and swirled in screams and whispers. His skin burned and froze from dust and moisture particles in the air. Scents of tilled earth, unwashed flesh, penned animals, and boiling food made him sick.

A knot of citizens appeared and pointed as he swayed, confounded by the physical and mental assault. The people spoke wearing wide-eyed and bewildered expressions. Fear and wonder also showed on some faces.

New sensations rocked Marcelo. The odor of hot, salty blood filled his nostrils as if he bathed in it. A multitude of beating hearts thundered in a mad tempo. An abrupt pang of hunger shook his body. Mouth watering, his stomach churned in starvation. His parched tongue and throat screamed for blood, to satiate the intense deprivation of sustenance.

Instinct conquered him, and he moved in a trance. He raced toward a woman and bit the side of her neck before she realized he was upon her. Most of the gathered citizens screamed and ran. Others pounded Marcelo using fists, rocks, and tools, but he ignored the attacks.

The female's warm, nourishing blood poured into his mouth. His throat worked in fervent swallows. The fire inside him raged in thirst. He crushed her body in a tight grip as if she might flee, yet the woman had already grown limp in his arms. He finally released his hold and she fell. Her eyes remained open and unseeing in death.

Exhilaration forced a shout of pleasure from Marcelo. He threw his head back and stared at the blazing stars embedded in the black tapestry of night. The hot blood coursed inside him like a potent fuel. His muscles thrummed, and bones quivered in a pleasurable buzz. An immense feeling of power and invulnerability swept over him. He could leap over a mountain or sprint across the jungle in a matter of moments. He could slaughter these people and feast on their blood. Nothing could stop him; the world became his to dominate and control.

A stone hit the back of his head and shattered his musing. A few Incas had remained, shouting and brandishing weapons. A cluster of weeping females lifted the dead woman. Realization stunned Marcelo and dropped him to his knees.

"What have I done?" he asked in a tremble.

Someone lunged and a beam of wood cracked against his head, but he barely felt it. He wiped his mouth and gaped at the blood stains on his fingers. Revulsion roiled his insides, and he dry-heaved. Guilt crushed his mind, and he screamed in rage.

Standing, he ran to the group of women and wrestled the lifeless female from their arms. He rocked her body and wailed in desperation and sorrow. How old was she? Did she have children? How would her parents feel? He sobbed into her neck, on the very spot where his teeth had ripped open her flesh.

The attacks on Marcelo had stopped, and the group stared in confusion. He handed the deceased woman back to the others, then turned and ran as fast as he could. Wind roared in his ears. The terrain blurred beneath his feet. Trees flew past in streaks of dark color. The sky moved in rapid bands of black swirled with white light. Marcelo didn't care how he moved at this incredible speed. He only wished to outrun the terrible ache cutting him deep inside.

The jungle eventually thinned as he raced through pastures dotted by shrubs and small thickets. He ran until the first rays of dawn broke the darkness on the eastern horizon. The rising sunlight burned his eyes and seared his skin. Hissing in pain, he sprinted into a patch of trees and collapsed in the cold morning shade.

Was he truly alive, or had he died back in that old man's hut? Did he now exist in a hellish afterlife where the sun threatened to turn him to ash? Why did his senses scream and pound in his head? Even now, he heard a bird flap its wings hundreds of feet in the air and detected the insects crawling through the field around him. His strength had also increased, and his body endured brutal attacks by the villagers leaving hardly a mark. His unnatural movements proved fluid and agile, implausible speed soaring him across the countryside in moments.

And the blood. Why had he craved it so much that his life screamed in jeopardy without it?

"I am so sorry," he whispered, thinking of the dead woman in his arms.

You will drink blood again.

The sudden voice boomed in Marcelo's head, and he shouted in alarm. Distraught and irrational, he thought he could escape the unexpected words. He sprinted out of the thicket and screamed as the sun charred his flesh. Madness taunted him as he stumbled back under the tree canopy in pain.

He later woke to a nighttime breeze and the music of crickets in the grass. A crescent moon drifted among the stars, the darkness welcome as it allowed him to travel. With no purpose or destination, Marcelo ran north in a blur of speed until the sun peeked its harmful rays over the landscape once more. For days, he followed the coast through ever-changing terrain and climate until it seemed he had run for over a thousand *leguas*, or leagues.

During this time, no hunger or thirst plagued him. He moved with swiftness and strength in his stride. His sharp senses adjusted to the environment around him. The volatile sounds, touch, and smell no longer tortured him through uncontrolled impressions and exaggerated awareness. Alone in the wilderness, he learned to adapt to and discern the various noises, powerful feelings, and shifting ambiences. He molded his new abilities and accepted them as part of his new life. Even though Marcelo failed to understand what had happened to him, he realized that indeed life remained—although his heart no longer beat and he had not drawn a breath since leaving that hut.

The blood-hunger returned on the seventh day. Marcelo had made it to Tenochtitlan, the ancient city of the Aztecs he had heard about that was conquered by another Spanish Conquistador, Hernan Cortes. On the ground, he writhed in the shadows outside the fallen city as devastating hunger gnawed his belly. He opened his mouth in anguish and exposed long canine teeth to the night sky. Nearing insanity, he rolled over and slammed his fists into the earth.

Drink, you fool! Blood is your life now.

That mysterious voice again. It compelled him with its simplicity and hard truth—Marcelo would die if he didn't ingest blood. He smelled it from the city teeming with subjugated natives and many armored Spaniards. The memory of pure exhilaration he had experienced from the Inca woman's blood swelled him with intense desire. He gave in to the voice, surrendered to sheer *need,* and slunk into the streets of Tenochtitlan.

Hundreds of potted fires and torches illuminated the enormous walled precincts, several palaces, and sprawling marketplaces. As a Conquistador serving under Francisco Pizarro, Marcelo could have found one of the officers and invented a story about being lost or reassigned. He would then be assigned back into the Spanish ranks having a roof over his head, food, and a chance to return home to his mother.

However, Marcelo was no longer the same person he had been upon leaving Spain. Still pondering his new condition, he doubted humanity even existed within him anymore. He thought of the smoke-demon seeping into his chest and understood that creature lurked inside, a separate entity yet part of Marcelo's very existence. His memories and thoughts endured, but his insane new abilities and bloodlust would always make him a dangerous target to society no matter where he wandered.

In the end, he might hurt someone he loved.

"I am sorry, Mama," he said, a knot of grief buried in his chest. "I love you and miss you so much."

Marcelo moved in the shadows and wasted no time looking for prey. He rounded the corner of a small temple that had been converted into a military barracks for Conquistadors, and nearly collapsed from hunger.

Shaking off the dizziness and summoning strength, he slipped through the door and pounced on a sleeping *soldado,* then sank his sharp canines into the man's neck.

A brief struggle on the cot woke an additional Spanish soldier, but Marcelo had already drunk his fill. Someone shouted an alarm and a torch roared to life. Weapons rattled as roused men leapt from their beds. Marcelo dashed out of the barracks and disappeared beyond the boundaries of the once great Aztec capital.

He continued north for several more days, halting under cover when the sun blazed and traveling great distances at night. Spanish explorers, traders, and missionaries were just beginning to venture into this wild and unexplored region of the Americas. However, Marcelo mainly encountered native tribes. Chumash, Pomo, and Chinook ruled in the west. As he traveled midland to further explore this terrain and somehow find peace under his new reality, Marcelo met the Apache and Navajo. Moving east, he came across the Comanche, Chickasaw, and Cherokee nations.

In the wilderness of North America, decades passed as he fed and grieved in a repetitious pattern of life. He had no home and no point to his mad existence. Enemies hunted him as a monster, devil, demon, night terror, or other names in a dozen languages. A few sympathetic acquaintances offered him shelter. Over the years he found no answer to what he had become, why it happened, or what he was supposed to do.

The wilderness transformed as exploration and society advanced. Modes of travel improved, and new technology exploded. Marcelo roamed the continents across the globe and eventually met other supernatural beings. A massive weight rose from his shoulders as relief from not being alone filled him. He traveled, loved, and wept some more. But most of all, he adapted and moved on with his life.

After a few centuries, Marcelo chose the United States to call home. And a peaceful, modern existence flew out the window the day he met Sybil Radella Cotterill…

Chapter Twenty-Two

Preparations

A few days later, Sybil sat in the breakfast nook eating a delicious plate of bacon, tots, and scrambled eggs with shredded cheese on top. Marcelo's kitchen had been fully stocked with "humanoid food" as he put it, and she had cooked herself a hearty meal to start the day.

Marcelo hovered over the stove and sprayed detergent to wipe up the mess Sybil had made. She had meant to clean up after herself…really! His wonderful home by the beach looked too immaculate for her to cause disorder. She would try to be more attentive and tidier during her daily routines, including not clogging up the drain with her strands of hair.

The rest and recovery had done wonders for Sybil's mind and body. Marcelo had recuperated as well; the wound from the branch impaling his torso had vanished. More importantly, long conversations had strengthened their relationship to restore the trust that Sybil had broken.

Waking from her three-hundred-year slumber, explosive rage had been the strongest emotion pushing her. Vengeance had fueled her desperate need to enact justice for Constance, and for her mother as well. Nothing else had mattered. Not even Sybil's health, friendships, or the safety of others.

The respite had soothed her raging mind and warring sentiments. She now experienced a much better perspective concerning the grave situation with Umaq. The danger encompassed the entire world and many innocent people, not just her personal life and selfish reasons for revenge. She had abandoned recklessness and would uphold the greater good after Marcelo and Grace had shown her the way.

After finishing her meal, she went into the master bedroom and found Marcelo folding laundry. On the wall, she observed the certificates and plaques awarded to him by various cities across the country. Each gift held an inscription describing his selfless contributions to the community. The words spoke of improved schools, libraries, hospitals, police, fire departments, and how life for the citizens had been enhanced by his efforts.

"Always the hero," she said with a smile.

"Hardly," he responded. He folded the last shirt and tucked it inside a drawer.

Sybil stepped toward Marcelo and slipped into his arms. "You are one to me, I warrant," she mumbled against his chest.

He kissed the top of her head. "Did you have enough to eat?"

She gazed into his young, ageless face, and nodded. "Yet you have not." She lifted her arm to press the palm of her hand against his lips.

"Take," she whispered.

He moved his mouth away. "No," he said softly.

"You need it, and I desire it. Take forth every part of me, Marcelo. Truly, I am yours."

Marcelo hadn't ingested blood in several days, and he appeared paler than usual. Conflicting emotions passed through his eyes and over his smooth features. She could tell he warred with his conscience—his body needed blood, yet his mind insisted this was wrong.

"Sybil…"

Marcelo closed his green eyes and gently bit her hand. She hissed in a breath as blood flowed into his mouth, though no pain accompanied the sensation. He pressed her against his body and her mind and spirit separated from the world. Her lifeforce roared in her ears with each beat of her heart as it provided him sustenance. He lifted her and she floated in wonder, skin tingling and toes curling in bliss.

Marcelo opened his eyes, his intense gaze ignited by passion. He pivoted toward the bed and lay Sybil upon it. A tentative hand explored her body as he lay next to her. He then drew back a bit, hesitating as if ashamed of his sudden advances. The situation had flown past simply drawing blood out of necessity. A spark had burst between them, a catalyst with the potential to summon an inferno.

With her face flushed and heart thundering, Sybil welcomed his soft touch…and more. Before, they had only ever kissed and held each other. But after everything they had been through—hammered by every emotion— Sybil burned to be with Marcelo in every way possible.

She cupped the back of his neck and pulled him close for a deep kiss. After undressing each other, Sybil clung to his body in desperate need and latched onto his essence in powerful desire. She sensed his equal hunger through each kiss and caress, his motions filled with longing as if she might run away again. Sybil swam in elation as she experienced Marcelo in a different, yet similar form of binding as in the blood studio. This time, no blood flowed; only emotions poured, their minds and bodies united in the act of love.

***

Afterwards, the pair held each other on the sofa and turned on the TV to catch any news about Umaq and Machu Picchu. They had waited for a sign since arriving in Avila Beach, and today the frenzied reporter from Peru did not disappoint. The chaotic scene on the television filled Sybil with dread as she held Marcelo's hand in a tight grip.

A news helicopter aired video of the ancient Inca city of Machu Picchu. Outside the city, wreckage of fighter jets and attack helicopters burned on the side of the mountain. Within the walls, a massive collection of demons swarmed the rich green fields and stone courtyards. Some of the creatures moved like ants, lifting stones and wood to rebuild the old city. Other monstrosities patrolled the perimeter while crawling or flying on leathery wings.

The live feed switched to a base camp set at the foot of the mountain. Amid a sea of green tents, soldiers from various countries hurried about carrying weapons and supplies. Military trucks and forklifts drove in the background. Near the command tent, the reporter stood with microphone in hand.

"A dangerous group of witches and demons have taken over the ancient ruins of Machu Picchu, the popular tourist destination in the country of Peru," the woman began. "Any attempt to breach the area has been met with fierce violence. Several military aircraft have been struck down, and foot soldiers struggling to reach the peak suffered heavy attack.

"The invaders are well-organized and operating under high intelligence. Our cameras managed to capture footage of who is believed to be the mastermind behind all this, an unidentified male at the center of the activity." A video of an earlier recording played with a camera zoomed in and centered on Umaq. He spoke amid a group of various demons and robed witches with Cessani close by.

"This is what we expected," Marcelo said as the feed cut back to the live reporter while she continued her story. "Soon Umaq will attempt to open the portal to the netherworld and summon even more demons."

"I warrant we shall need an army of our own," Sybil responded. She shook her head at the TV. "Truly, this is madness."

Marcelo stood from the sofa and paced across the rug. "I'm going to contact two associates of mine. I can only hope at least one of them will join us."

"Who do you have in mind?"

Marcelo smiled. "Oh, just your typical werewolf and a dryad."

"You have interesting friends, and a fair sight our group would be," Sybil said, standing. "My heart only hopes everything shall fare well."

He took her into his arms, and she closed her eyes. "As long as we're together, I know we'll be fine," he said softly.

For the moment, only Marcelo's comforting words mattered. With his love she had found courage, purpose, and the power to protect those she cared about.

A dark, momentous war lay ahead. Untold perils awaited Sybil and her companions. But she vowed to be their light, a foundation of strength and resolve to stop Umaq and his demons.

About the Author

Alexander Fernandez is a multi-award-winning author whose work has been featured in *Kirkus Reviews* magazine. He was born in Santa Monica, CA and grew up in Rancho Cucamonga. Retired from the United States Air Force after serving 24 years, he lives with his wife Helem in Roseville.

Alex has been writing fantasy and paranormal stories since early childhood for both school and for pleasure. He hopes to make a lasting emotional impact in his readers. He thrives in the exhilaration of creating memorable characters and adventures that become a part of the reader's life.

ADDITIONAL BOOKS BY THIS AUTHOR IN EPIC FANTASY:

Lonely World Trilogy

Book One: Tears for a World
Book Two: Tears for Love
Book Three: Tears for Life